Short Bus

Short Bus

Brian Allen Carr

Texas Review Press
Huntsville, Texas

FIRST EDITION, 2011
Requests for permission to reproduce material from this
work should be sent to:

Permissions
Texas Review Press
English Department
Sam Houston State University
Huntsville, TX 77341-2146

Acknowledgements:

Some of the stories in this collection initially appeared
in Boulevard, DogzPlot, elimae, Gigantic, Keyhole
Magazine, NOO 12, NANO Fiction, Pindeldyboz,
SmokeLong Quarterly, Texas Review, Thieves Jargon,
3:AM Magazine.

Cover design by Justin Sirois

Library of Congress Cataloging-in-Publication Data
Carr, Brian Allen, 1979-
  Short bus / Brian Allen Carr. -- 1st ed.
     p. cm.
  ISBN 978-1-933896-54-0 (pbk. : alk. paper)
  1. Lower Rio Grande Valley (Tex.)--Fiction. 2. Mexican-
American Border Region--Fiction. I. Title.
  PS3603.A772S55 2010
  813'.6--dc22
                                         2010040192

In Memory of William Patrick Carr

(1977-2000)

Contents

Short Bus

RUNNING THE DRAIN

I'll check the police report in the morning from Mexico. I'll slip across the border at Reynosa. I'll buy a cheap, rusted car and a pistol and drive south. I'll get a room in the mountains. I'll walk through the pines and kick fallen needles. I'll be free. I'll think about the fire and my finger prints and the neighbors and the severed corpses in the bath tub with blood running the drain. Was it sloppy? Was I sloppy? The mountains will not hold me long with my money. That is the place money goes to burn. I'll jump a bus to the coast of Tampico. I'll rent a palapa and lay in a hammock in the shade. I'll drink quarts of Corona with slices of lime. In the evenings the woman at the inn will slaughter a chicken and roast it over an open flame. The skin will crack and pop as the coals burn bright red below. When the bird is cooked she'll wrap it in foil. I'll buy half the chicken. She'll bring me a plate of onions, cilantro and lime. She'll bring me corn tortillas and grilled serrano peppers. I'll eat giant mouthfuls, sucking down beer and salty air between bites. I'll sleep with the innkeeper's daughter. Her teenaged body already mature. She'll smell like cinnamon toasting in a cast-iron pan. My hammock will sway with our sex. I will not stay in Tampico. The beach is corrosive. I'll take another bus to Oaxaca City. I'll walk the streets eating chipulenes. Fried grasshoppers with chili and lime. I'll look at the artwork. Great art in Oaxaca. I'll get a room at a good hotel. I'll unpack my luggage into drawers.

I'll look at her dress. Why did I keep it? Will I put it on? I'll wait for dusk. I'll shave my face, chest and legs. I'll enter the street in her dress. I'll call myself by her name. I'll walk slow by the men. I'll hold them in my eyes. They will look at me in turn. They will not know of the bodies. Of the blood. The fire. The drain. If I'm lucky they will take the bait. They will talk to me in their language, their lips moving calm beneath mustaches in the dusk. They will buy me sweet drinks on a patio bar. They will ignore my throat, which will give me away. I will hold my face in my hand. I'll smile when they tell jokes. A language so floral. They will take me in horse buggies to the barrios that ache with age. They will take me to their empty homes. They will show me their guitars and sing boleros softly. When the time is right I will take what I came for. I won't feel sorry for the sad faces trembling. They should have spotted my disease. They should have sensed how I could learn them.

2

NOT HEARING THE JINGLE

In the old yard adjacent the high school sat a green-metal box that housed an emergency generator. At least we always said it did, though I've unlearned plenty since those days. Used to we'd hang there after school, waiting, though I'm not sure for what. Faces, the names I knew, those kids, they mostly footed it home, as we all lived close to campus. I can't fathom it now, but must've been we'd a reason to toil there, in those hot afternoons, the yard so dry from sun, the sky an anemic sheet of cloudless blue sprawled above. I remember the wind stained by white dust that'd blow in from the parched citrus orchard beyond, so the air, powdered and grainy, struck your eyes as an accident may, as though the world would swing up like a mess of barbed wire uncoiled from its post. A girl. Sally Mixon. Atop the box. Her feet dangling, kicking a bit, drumming against the green-sheet metal, a smile on her face wide as a sunset, her shoulders pumping like alternating bolls in the wind. She sang a bit of song. Something I know I knew at the time but now can't remember. An upbeat thing. She smiled, and then, as rows cross, our eyes, loose with immaturity, touched from their distance, and my shoulders got hotter than a summer-time scarecrow's, and her face went red as the clay could, and then a washing, no water, but a washing, the way air from a cold building cleans you of heat in the doorway, though I know the temperature didn't change. I remember

3

thinking, at the moment, that something would come. I put a hand in my blue-jean pocket and shucked my shoulder, confident, waiting for words from her. But silence. A hollow. And I kept throwing my eyes at her, but for nothing, no connection, like trying to fish dropped keys from a blind crevice with a clothes hanger and not hitting the ring. Not hearing the jingle.

When I'm alone, just me and the pillow, the fan blade above swinging, between the clock telling me to bed down and the alarm telling me to rise up, I wrack my mind for the song. The tune of it sillies me, and time wisps away, and I can't find a name to call it. For a while I thought, if I heard it again, I could hunker down like a fresh-ginned bundle and quit moving forever.

My bartender heard me on the subject a time too many and slammed a telephone book down in front of me and asked me if the girl was from around here, because no one from these parts ever moves on, and that I could probably find her or her folks, call her up and just get it over with. Said he was sick of me half in the bag with a quarter in my hand, flipping through albums in the jukebox and never picking a song. Said that when I'm deep in the liquor I drag strangers by their arms to the stool aside me and hum at them and ask if they know the tune, and when they stare back puzzled I hum it again. Said it was pathetic. Embarrassing. But faced with it that way it seemed part of me didn't want to know. Truth isn't always kind to memory.

I met an Argentinean immigrant at a cantina in the border town of Nuevo Progresso, which sits right on the Rio Grande about an hour's drive from the Gulf. It's a heap held together by tourist's dollars. Mexicans selling cheap blankets on the sidewalks, and knock-off name-brand purses, and watches, and sun glasses, and seven-year-olds running around selling gum or begging nickels. I was down there with a friend who said he knew a place a fella could buy a blow job, but we just went to a strip club that had porn playing on lots of TV screens and had women loafing around that looked like nieces of gas-station attendants or like they worked part-time changing tires, and I wouldn't pay to touch them. My friend must've though, because he disappeared for a stretch, came back grinning, and he was whistling when we walked away. The Argentinean stumbled up to us in the next bar we stopped. He was a tiny, tanned thing with ears like empty leather gloves. He asked for a cigarette, and I gave him one and shook his hand. His fingers like the tines of a baby pitchfork. Sprawled, gnarly and firm. He sat with us a minute blowing smoke rings and swilling tequila, and we got to talking about the Pampas, and how they look like South Texas, and I asked when's the next time he'd be going back, but he shook his head no. He said too many years had passed since his last trip and that if he went back now, and saw his old friends, how they'd gotten on, and he was surrounded by their age, all those ears like empty gloves and baby-pitchfork handshakes, that it'd drought him of his youth.

A couple of months back I saw Sally Mixon from her blind side walking the rows of a carniceria—a Mexican butcher shop that sells beef cuts white folks consider scraps for grind. She had a child with her and I sort of followed, her body beyond bloom, spread out like worn cloth. I don't think she saw me. I kept my head low till she left and then bought some cheeks to braise. I wonder how it'd have done me if I'd heard her voice. If I'd gone up and said hello? What would she think of me, and I of her? Would she think that my face had weathered? Would I think that her eyes had dried? Would she notice my dipped shoulders and pouting belly, and I her flaccid arms and sagging throat? Would we stand there in the smell of meat, the fluorescents humming and the air-conditioned air and the soft lull of a corrido crackling through a radio speaker from somewhere behind the butcher's counter? Would she introduce me to the child? Would I know the child's father? Would I ask her about the song? Would she even remember? Could she sing it? Could she sing it to me then? And would her voice make fade the smell of beef blood and fill the store with powdery sunlight? Or would she sing it, and nothing, her voice lost in the fluorescent hum, her arms jiggling at her sides? And in finishing the tune would we be swallowed by a difficult silence, our face muscles heavy, our skin hot, left with no option but to push our carts towards aisles of opposite direction, and would the old memory be dulled for me?

Last week they harvested the cotton fields. I parked my car and watched the machines offloading the haul. It's been a stretch of years since I've done that work. Now I sublet the land and take a percent of the yield. My father though, he was a farmer. He used to come down with a thermos of coffee and work alongside the hands and try to keep them straight. But I've never been keen on it. The best part of the harvest is when it's over and the tufts of cotton that blow off the bails litter the field edges like mounds of old snow. Once I asked my dad why we didn't have the hands pick up the blow off and add it to the rest of the haul, but he spit and told me small things are easier to let lie. Of course he didn't always follow his code. Once he got to arguing with a Mexican hand over eighteen dollars difference in day's wages, and my father got mad and threw out a cup of coffee, and I don't think he meant it, but it splashed against the hand's son's face, and then the man pulled a knife and sliced my father's throat and he fell to his knees and bled to death on a bale. Died before an ambulance could come. I watched it, but I can't really remember what I saw. Red I guess. Some flailing. I was a few yards away. I do remember watching the hand run after he'd cut him. He dragged his son by the arm and they headed away from the road. Slipped over a few fences and ran deep into farmland. But the law caught them within the day. The father they sent to Huntsville where he was put to death. The son they roughed up a bit, but he still lives in town. I see him from time to time. My guess is he picks cotton, same as his dad did. He always tips his hat at me.

Barry Hannah
Airships

Chuck Kinder

OVER THE BORDER

Holt pulled the Jeep into a gas station on a long stretch of pale-grassy road that was split by a median planted with palm trees. They were the only palms on the plain. East toward the gulf and west, further the mainland, the pale grass was dotted with knotty mesquite and yellow-needle pierced cactus.

"I gotta piss," Holt said. "Anyone else?"

Jardon and Trotter shook their heads no, so Holt went in alone. He passed a bum on the way into the store who held his palms out to Holt as though asking him to wait and listen, but Holt dropped a shoulder, skirted him, and went inside. Then the bum moved toward the Jeep. He looked like he'd stood to close to a fire. His face grime smeared, his hands grey, his clothes seemed slathered with oyster liquor, as though they'd gone wet and dry several times against his skin.

"What you think?" Trotter asked Jardon.

"Why not?" Jardon said, and Trotter let down his window.

"Need something?"

"Sir, here's the deal," said the bum, his voice squeaking like a cork being pulled from a bottle. "I could tell from over there that you's a Christian, and that's what I am, I'm Christian," the bum pulled up a sleeve to show a crooked cross tattooed on his shoulder. "And I'm in a bit of a bind, you see, cause I got a wife and kid, and they's been in a van down the road here for two days, cause we ran out of gas

8

coming back from a missionary trip building houses in northern Mexico for homeless, and they've just been stranded out there, and I'm trying to get some scratch together, you see, so I can go back down with a tank of gas, and drive em on home."
"Well," said Trotter, and he looked down the road. "It's pretty rough country. Illegals. Coyotes. Border patrol."
"I know," said the bum.
"If your family's been stuck in a van up the road for a few days there's a good chance they're arrested, dying or dead."
"Well, as soon as I get some money I'm aim to go see," the bum said.
"Yeah," said Trotter, "but I'd hate to waste money on something like gas for two dead folks in a van."
"I see," said the bum, and he tapped his lips with a finger. "But what if I promised, maybe, just to use the money on me like. You know, just move on?"
"There's an idea," Trotter said. He smiled at the bum and rolled up the window and Jardon laughed. Then the bum held up his grey middle fingers at Trotter, and he was still holding them up when Holt stepped back out of the store.
"What's going on?" Holt said.
The bum looked over his shoulder at Holt, and Trotter lowered his window half way.
"Guy needs money to save his dying family up the road."
"Really," said Holt, and he looked the man up and down.
"Yes, sir, it's true," said the bum. "They're just up yonder," he pointed down the road.
"Wait," said Trotter, "I thought you said they were the other direction."
The bum made a puzzled face and glanced down the road both ways. "Well, hell," he said. "Must've got turned round."

"What you think?" Holt asked. "Should we help him?"

"Don't know," said Trotter. "He says he's Christian."

"My mother's Christian," Holt said.

"Well there you go," said the bum. "We got to help each other out and that, like in the book."

"Sure," said Holt. "How much you need?"

"Whatever you can spare, I guess."

Holt reached for his wallet, took it from his jeans and held it gentle in his hand as though it were a living thing. The bum eyed the wallet. "But here's the deal," said Holt, "I take issue with just giving money away."

"Sure," he answered. "I understand. I'll do something for it."

"Like what?" said Holt.

The bum surveyed the plain. Across the lot, at the edge of the grass, stood a Nopal Cactus with prickly fruit growing from its needled paddles. "Ever had a prickly pear?" he asked and pointed at the cactus.

Holt looked at the cactus. "A what?"

"I'll show you," he said. "Come with me."

Holt and the bum passed across the asphalt lot toward the edge of plain, where, surrounded by pale grass, the aggressive cactus, its green paddles fierce, sprawled like an upside down squid, its limbs pointing skyward. At the tips of the paddles, the pears, like the noses of clowns, red, so red as though filled with blood, and dry from the sun, skin flaking and fine needles. There were nearly a dozen of them.

"How many you want?" said the bum, and he pointed at the fruit.

"Oh," said Holt, "I guess I'll say when."

The bum smiled. "Sure thing," he said, and he tiptoed toward the cactus. Holt moved behind him. The bum looked over his shoulder. "You coming in with me?" he asked.

"Well," said Holt, "it's just that I've never s
it done is all."

"It's nothing," he said. "Watch."

The bum moved into the sprawl of paddles
and reached for one of the bright-red fruit, gently
with the tips of his fingers, and taking it pulled
the bud down and toward him, so it snapped away
clean from the paddle, and he held it in his hand.
He turned to look at Holt and grinned, and a string
of saliva slipped from the side of the bum's mouth.
He dried his lips on his shoulder before setting the
fruit in Holt's hand.

"Just a couple more," Holt said and motioned
toward the Jeep. "You know, for the fellas."

"No problem, sir," he said. "It'll be my
pleasure."

The bum smiled, kind of bowed, then turned and
moved toward another fruit, his arm stretched long.

"Wait," said Holt.

"Yes, sir," the bum said and turned.

"Why don't you get us those two," said Holt,
and he pointed to a pair of pears deep in the
paddles. "Those ones look best."

"Of course," said the bum, and he smiled and
bowed again. Then he turned to make his way into
the nest of needles. Moving slowly, he raised a
foot, his balance swayed and he held out his hands.
That's when Holt kicked. He reared back like a
punter and struck the bum's ass hard with the toe of
his shoe, sending the grimy man face first into the
spiky paddles, and the bum hollered as he thumped
through the plant and toward the ground. His shirt
tore on the way down, and he screamed when his
body thumped the dirt. "Mother fucker. My face."

Holt ran back to the Jeep. Trotter threw open
the door for him, and Holt jumped in, and tossed
the pear to Jardon. "It's fruit," he said. He turned
the keys, the starter grinding as the bum screamed
from the cactus.

11

Jardon bit the pear. "Tastes like tomato," he said, then spit into his hand, "but it's fucking thorny."

Holt pulled alongside the cactus.

"My face. I'll fucking kill you." The bum had one hand to his face and was wrestling through the cactus, grabbing at paddles with his free hand to help himself up, then pulling it away and shaking it as though he'd touched a hot pan.

"That don't sound Christian," said Holt. Then Jardon leaned into the front seat and threw the bit pear. It hit the bum good in the throat and he fell back into the paddles screaming. Holt mashed the gas. The Jeep's tires whined against the asphalt. They turned and were back on the highway moving south.

Earlier that day:

Holt sunk his foot on the clutch, revved the engine, and the Jeep shuddered as exhaust clipped through leaks at the engine's headers and the tires ground deeper into the loose gravel of the lot. Ahead a small restaurant stood. Brown brick and copper roof. A kitchen door, opened save the screen, with silhouettes moving behind it like fish shadows swimming falsely on the surface of a murky shallow.

"He said five minutes," Holt said, and hit the throttle again.

"Hold up," said Trotter. "It'll be soon."

Trotter was growing a mustache. He touched it with his fingers as though he wanted it wiped away, flicking the spare hairs with the prints of his fingers, first with, then against the grain. A faint noise like static from a record player before the music starts. Holt reached up, grabbed the passenger visor and flipped it down, so Trotter's face shown back at him in the mirror. "Tell me it looks good," Holt said.

Trotter let his eyes lay lazily on his reflection, then he wiped the visor closed with the back of a hand. "It'll fill," he said and licked his fingers.

Trotter stared beyond his half-opened window fingering his thin mustache as Holt shook his head and revved the engine once more, slapping his palms against the steering wheel as the RPM needle floated back down to one.

"Look it," Trotter said and pointed.

Across the lot the screen door opened, and a round Mexican man with thin-slit eyes limped out onto the gravel, kicking pebbles and waving at the Jeep.

"You know this cat?" Holt asked.

"I've seen him," Trotter said. "One of Jardon's bosses."

The Mexican smiled, his dark-brown lips drawn tight toward his ears, breathing heavy as he moved, so his breath hissed over the Jeep's idling engine, and his paper-white chef jacket heaved on his shoulders. He pulled a crumpled towel from his back-left pocket and rubbed it across his sweaty face and neck. Trotter looked at Holt, and Holt shrugged his shoulders. Trotter lowered his window completely as the Mexican leaned against the Jeep.

"Afternoon," said the Mexican.

"Hey," Holt said and nodded. Trotter slouched in his seat.

"You taking this little motherfucker with you?" The Mexican waved his palm at the kitchen.

"Depends if he can come," said Holt.

"Yeah," said the Mexican, and he put a thumb up toward the kitchen. "It'll be slow. Not too many dishes. We'll give him off." The Mexican reached a burly hand toward his thick mustache and combed it with his fingers. He looked at Trotter's lips. He nodded and smiled.

Holt dropped the Jeep into neutral. "Anything we can help you with?"

"Sure," the Mexican said and toweled his face. "Take good care of this little motherfucker." He pointed at the kitchen, "Cause he's," the Mexican touched the side of his head with a finger, "you know." The screen door of the kitchen opened and Jardon walked backwards through it.

"Yeah," said Holt. "We know," he nodded at the Mexican and eyed Jardon's backwards walk. "Can't promise nothing other than we'll try."

The Mexican wiped his face. "All I ask."

A throaty man in a button up and tie appeared in the kitchen door and leaned against the jam, looking on as Jardon turned and made way through the gravel.

"Who's that?" Trotter asked.

"Manager," said the Mexican.

"He's looking funny at us," Trotter said.

The Mexican smiled and looked toward the door. "He no like mustaches," the Mexican said. He nudged Trotter with his elbow, smiled at Jardon, then patted the dishwasher on the shoulder as he climbed in the backseat.

Trotter watched the manager pull his tie away from his throat and step back into the kitchen. The Mexican smiled, moved away from the Jeep and waved his towel. He pointed to the side of his head and looked at Holt. Holt laughed and geared the transmission. The Mexican waved his towel again, and Holt drove toward the street.

Trotter watched his palms as the Jeep drove southwest following the course of the Oso inlet which fingered its salty way land bound from Corpus Christi Bay and dwindled to a shallow bit of brackish grass-laden creek where men in torn clothes cast nylon nets into the water, a river also called Oso, that twisted northeast, just as the Jeep would, then faded to a trickle, near the same spot the Jeep turned south and paralleled the Texas coast heading toward Mexico.

"Feel it now?" Holt asked.

Trotter shook his head and looked across the fields of cotton, his vision fanning through the rows blinking by, so the same view, lines of dirt rows between cotton, traveled with the Jeep, and he pressed his hands together, lining up his fingers and mashing his palms. He moved in his seat. He thumbed his thin mustache. He turned an air-condition vent away from his face. "Comes and goes," he said.

Holt nodded and looked in the rearview mirror at Jardon who was rifling through his backpack. "Don't even think about smoking back there," Holt said.

"I wasn't going to," said Jardon.

Then Holt smiled in the rearview mirror. "What do you think?" he asked.

"Bout what?" said Jardon.

"Bout Trott's stache?"

Jardon leaned his head across the front seat to give a look, but Trotter turned his face away. "It's not hiding anything, if that's the point," Jardon said.

Trotter touched a finger to the cleft where the lobes of his upper lip had been doctored together and looked like two knuckles of a limp fist. "Not trying to," Trotter said.

"Then what's the point?"

"Not sure," Trotter said, and he dragged his bottom teeth across his cleft lip. "Just trying something I guess." He dragged the teeth.

Holt smiled. Jardon reached across the front seat and thumped Trotter's shoulder. Someone turned on the radio.

*　　　*　　　*

Once Holt asked Trotter what it was like.

"You ever thought about a word?"

"Is that a real question?"

"Yeah it's a real question."

"Like before you look it up in the dictionary?"

"No, like a word that you'd never look up in a dictionary, a word that you've always known."

"Why would I think about a word that I know?"

"I don't know," Trotter said. "Just thinking about the way it's spelled, or the way you move the tongue to say it, or why it means what it does."

"I don't get it."

"Like quarter."

"Money?"

"Sure, or like a quarter piece of pie."

"Sure, quarter."

"Like, you've never taken a word like quarter, and said it so many times, and slow, said it slow, so your mouth had to think about moving the muscles to get it out, and your ears heard your voice being made against your vocal chords, and you started to think about all the other words it sounds like. Like water. And why quarter kind of sounds like water when they're not the same thing at all. Or daughter, or fodder, or whatever. And you say quarter a hundred and fifty eight times, and think about it so long, that you know it can't possibly mean what you think it's always meant, and that you've been wrong all your life, and just operating on bad information."

"I guess," Holt said. "Maybe a time or two, but I don't get what that has to do with the anxiety."

"It comes. I notice something too much," Trotter said. "The way it starts. Light on a table. Hum of an A/C. Once it was the aerator of a fish tank bubbling. Once I was sitting at a table in a restaurant on the second floor, and the floor must've been soft, or something, because every time a waiter walked by the floor shook beneath me, and my eyes bounced with the floor."

"So?"

"So then I get to thinking that I was set up funny, and that I don't hear and see right, and then it starts to feel like I'm moving backwards, or like I'm sitting still and everything else is moving away."

"For how long?"

"For however long it lasts. Sometimes I can figure it out. I find the source and it stops. Sometimes I've got to leave where I'm at. Go to the bathroom. Go out for air."

"How often?"

Trotter dragged his teeth across his cleft. "Almost every day I guess."

The fattest waiter. His face. Pelted flesh, black cheeks, nose coarse as a sponge. He rocked. Hull-bodied, his tuxedo tight sunk in his flesh, the way ropes around trees grow into the bark when the years pass. He handed out menus. Holt, Trotter and Jardon sat. They were hours from the coast of their departure, they'd threaded cotton fields, down further south the ranchland, squeezing into the citrus groves, the trees in rows with dark green leaves and bright orange fruit, tracts of land surrounded by trailer parks divided with dirt roads of poor drainage, so standing puddles, filthy water, lay breading grounds for minnow-sized mosquitoes though it hadn't rained for days. They'd crossed the bridge. "Is that it?" Suspended above the Rio Grande, chunks of loose sod flopping in the slow churning brown current beneath, and women with children, cross-legged on the walkway holding upside-down ball caps by their brims asking for change. Then guards, Mexican men in blue shirts absently waving the cars passed, because who would bring anything in, and soldiers, boys in olive-green jumpers and helmets, some aside the armored car and some behind the sandbags and all with machineguns and smiling at camera-toting tourists taking pictures and posing, because, after all, they're there for the safety anyway. Then the road. One. Town of Nuevo Progresso. One thoroughfare with unpaved tributaries fanning toward barrios, dirtier and more dilapidated the further from Benito Juarez Avenue, the musical street, with buildings painted so bright, like Easter eggs in the sunshine, a sweet liquor laid down by a paintbrush, so if you looked long enough you'd get drunk, and longer still nauseous and shaky off the yellow, fuchsia and turquoise. Away from the water. Away from the bridge. On either side the road, buildings and stands, cheap goods, though handmade, painted quick, priced to sell, and, "I give you good price," and, "No don't go away," and, "Almost free. Today. For you. Almost free," or, "Need a dentist? Pharmacy? To drink? Massage? Shoe shine? Haircut? My sister's only twelve. Window tint? Hammock? Bracelet for the pretty lady? Massage? Haircut? Today, almost free."

Holt and Jardon ordered. The waiter, with pen and pad in hand, watched Trotter patiently as he read the menu. Trotter dragged his teeth across his mustached cleft. "I don't know," he said. "What do you suggest?"

A few days ago, while watching TV, they'd seen a commercial. A woman sat in a crowded room that oscillated as she panicked. Voices, her friend's, her husband's, hollow and tinny, "Is something wrong? Something wrong?" The woman pushed away from the table, a set table, white cloth, crystal, china, candle light flickering, "Fine, just, I'm." Then moving. Her face, red dress, hands, losing color and the room pitching as though on an ocean voyage and she the fulcrum of the pitch.

Then the woman, black and white, in a frenzy of tossing color that surrounded her, voices turning to laughter and chasing from edges like paper being burned. Then the view, fading to white. Then just the screen, pure white. Then the name of a pill in a font so dark and bold that Jardon and Holt both said the name aloud and looked at Trotter who said he'd try anything once.

They stepped out of the restaurant and into the sun. Jardon picked at his tongue with his fingernails, then dragged the tip of his tongue across his front teeth, "Dam needles," he said and then mouthed a cigarette.

They moved along the crowded street single file. On one side of them booths, tabletops drowned with jewelry and knock-off name-brand sunglasses, on the other store fronts with salespeople urging them in. They worked along the smooth-worn cement, sliding their feet looking side to side. A young man stood, gold teeth and a white pharmacist's jacket, auctioning from a street corner, "Vitamins, heart burn medicine, antibiotics." Then, as the three moved closer, in a quieter voice, "Valium, painkillers, sleeping pills." The three stopped in front of him. The tag on his jacket said *Miguel*. He was holding a stack of yellow fliers.

"What you need?" Miguel asked.

Trotter took a piece of paper from his pocket and handed it to Miguel. Miguel motioned for them to follow, and he led them a few store fronts down to a pharmacy and walked them to the counter. Miguel gave the piece of paper to the clerk.

"We have generic," he said.

Holt, Jardon and Trotter looked confused.

"Same, but cheaper," said Miguel.

"We'll take it," said Trotter.

The clerk went to the end of the counter, climbed a step ladder, grabbed a white and orange box and came back to the register. He pressed a few buttons. "Nine dollar," he said.

"No shit," said Holt.

The clerk looked confused. Trotter gave him the money and took the box. "Better than insurance," he said and opened the box.

"Take when feel effects," said the clerk.

Trotter opened the box, took out the bottle, twisted off the top and popped a pill.

"Alright," said Jardon. "Now let's get down to it."

"Fine," Holt said, and he looked at Miguel. "Where should we go to have a good time?"

They left the Jeep parked on the busy street and headed away from the bridge on foot. There was a man with a cab there. Miguel said they'd know him. The music, the colors, the crowd all faded the farther from the river they walked. They could see beyond the main stretch to the rows of unfinished buildings with exposed rebar dangling like loose wires from the roofs. On the way they passed a butcher shop, slabs of beef in the windows and an old man standing outside at a copper pot, frying out pork skin, the smell, heavy as taint, painted their nostrils, and they stopped and watched the steam coming off the grease and beads of sweat slipped from their brows.

"Want?" the old man asked and stirred the pot with a giant wooden spoon.

"No thanks," said Jardon. "Just looking."

Then Holt spotted a liquor store and they went inside. Holt bought a small bottle of tequila, and they passed it around, and Jardon smoked a few cigarettes on the road before heading deeper toward the man with the cab.

They knew him when they saw him, he smiled big and opened a car door.

"Five-dollar pussy wagon," he said. "Fucky, fucky, sucky, suck."

The boys laughed and handed him a bill. Holt and Trotter climbed into the back seat and Jardon climbed into the front. They passed the bottle of tequila among the four of them as the car floated, loose shocks or no shocks at all, over the dusty streets, back deeper into Mexico.

The radio was playing some kind of drunken waltz, the driver sang along and held his hand like a pistol, and shiny things dangled from the review mirror.

They pulled to a wrought iron gate. The driver mashed the brakes, and the car slung to a stop, throwing coliche as its back tires kicked to the side.

"Thanks for the ride," Holt said.

The three climbed from the car and walked toward the gate and made their way into the district.

Whores. Oh, the whores. Their bodies beaten, drained like used batteries, so their forms held, but something in the eyes, a vacuous swallow of light rather than a twinkle, and a looseness of skin, so their bones seemed far away even as you stood beside them and eyed their smiles. They leaned in doorways to rooms that opened to the street, on either side, and the sun dipped toward an orange colored west, and a graying east, so the rooms, their pale light spilling, like twin strands of dirty Christmas lights pulled tight across a bed of dust. "What you want? Got what you need." And Holt, Jardon and Trotter loose eyed in the filth of it.

"Kids look lost," an old white man with spare teeth and a black cane said. "First time?"

"Yeah," said Holt. "Just here to look."

The old man smiled and thumped his cane against the dust. "Well, stay away from these then," the old man said and lifted his cane motioning to the rooms that lined the road. "There's bars down the road that're better suited for you."

"Thanks," said Holt, and the three walked down the dirty road, as the old man slipped into one of the dim-lit rooms and sang as his whore giggled.

At the end of the road two bars. The first, a near palace. Steps to a covered patio, and an ivory-colored door beneath an arch. On the patio a man stood, his hand holding a rope. On the end of the rope, a donkey, tied by the neck, wide eyed, and tail wagging. The second, an open-door ramshackle. Chipped-paint façade, sad music emitting. Dust. The building dusty, as though found in an attic, and a meager tiki torch speared through the dirt as a beacon. Next to the torch a frail man, head wrapped in a bandana, eating peanuts and dropping the shells, sitting on a stool, legs crossed, hand on chin, staring. Eyes glued to a midget-sized monkey in a cage.

"I say the joint with the donkey," Trotter said.

"No," said Jardon. "He said it was the one with the monkey."

Jardon walked ahead, and Trotter and Holt looked at each other. Holt shrugged and followed along. Trotter watched the donkey until Holt called his name from the door. Then he ran past the caged monkey and into the bar.

Jardon stood at the bar with his arms crossed.

"I don't want tequila," he said. "I don't want beer, or tequila, and I don't want rum."

"That's mostly what we got," said the bartender.

"You speak English," said Holt.

"Sure," the tender said. "Went to school on the other side."

"What else you got?" Jardon asked.

"I got whiskey."

"Got anything different?" asked Trotter. "Something we've never had?"

The bartender pursed his lips. "Got absinthe," he said, and pulled a bottle from beneath him. "Can't say I recommend it though. Kind of tastes like licorice."

"Give us three," said Holt, and he slapped a twenty dollar bill to the bar.

The bartender nodded, "Sure thing," he said. The bartender took three goblets from a cabinet. He dropped an ice cube in each goblet and poured the absinthe—feeble green—before placing slotted spoons on the mouths of each glass, and placing a cube of sugar on each spoon. He doused the cubes with more absinthe. He set the sugar cubes on fire. Trotter, Jardon and Holt lowered their faces to the flames. Then the tender took a bottle of water and poured the water on the cubes, and the sugar water hit the liquor, and it clouded and went jade, and the tender removed the spoons and said, "Drink it fast."

They grabbed their drinks and obeyed, chugging steadily until the drinks were gone.

"Tastes like shit," Jardon said and slammed down his glass.

"Not so bad," said Trotter, and he held his glass to a light.

Holt set his glass on the bar and stared at it. He licked his lips. The bartender brought him his change. It was a bill and some coins. Holt held the money in his hands. He looked at it. He moved his lips. He looked at Trotter. "Man," he said, "quarter's a fucked up word."

It was different than the strip clubs in the states. The girls came around to their table in the corner. The three sipped bottles of beer, and the girls would dance up to them and bare themselves and smile. "You like?" they'd ask, and, if someone did,

23

the girls would lead them to another corner, just as dimly lit, and down a hallway, to a stable of stalls with stools, where they would give the customer private dances that would go as far as the money allowed, but none of them had been down the hall.

A girl with a floppy hat came to the table. "You boys look lonely," she said.

"You speak English," said Holt.

"I went to school in America," she said.

"Like the bartender," said Trotter.

"Yes," she said. "He's my brother."

Trotter, Jardon and Holt looked at the bartender who waved at them.

"How'd you end up here?"

"You say it like it's bad," the girl said and smiled.

"Sorry," said Holt. "Didn't mean to." He smiled back at her.

Trotter took a sip of his beer. "What's it run?"

"It?" she said.

"Sure," said Trotter. "You know."

She smiled. "Depends what *it* is. Some things cost a bit. Tickles are a dollar." She stuck two fingers into Trotter's ribs and he smiled.

"Take me to where the other girls take boys," he said.

Jardon and Holt looked at Trotter. Holt put his arm across Trotter's chest, leaned in and whispered, "What are you doing?"

Trotter whispered back, "Just wanna see."

The girl led him down the hallway to a stall where she sat him on a stool. Trotter sipped his beer and watched her unbutton her shirt, then she straddled Trotter and pulled his face to her chest and rocked back and forth, so his cheeks wiped against her soft breasts. She giggled. "You're prickly," she said. She pushed his head back and looked at his face.

"I'm growing a mustache," he said. "What do you think?"

She touched the mustache with her fingers and felt his cleft. "Oh," she said. "I like." She grabbed either side of his lip with her fingers, and, taking them, slightly spread apart, leaned toward him, her lips spread, and flicked her tongue in his cleft.

Trotter leaned away. "What the fuck was that?" he asked.

"What?" she said and smiled.

"That. What you did," he said. "What was it?"

"Nothing," she said. "Just having fun."

Trotter brushed the girl off him and grabbed his pills from his pocket. He dragged his teeth across the cleft of his lip, opened the bottle and put a pill on his tongue. He took the pill with a swallow of beer, and headed down the hallway without giving the girl any money.

"Sorry," she screamed, but she didn't follow him.

Trotter came back to the table.

"How'd it go?" Holt asked.

Trotter didn't answer. "Be back in a minute," he said. He held up a finger, pointed at the door, then left the bar.

Trotter's mustache was gone when he came back to the table. "You can get anything you want out there," he said and smiled, but no one smiled back.

Holt was rubbing his head and Jardon was leaned back in his chair. Jardon made like he was going to say something, but Holt held up his hand and said, "Shut it," then he looked at Trotter, but he didn't say anything.

Trotter watched him for a while. "What?"

"The Mexican," Holt said.

"Which one?" Trotter asked.

"Javi," said Jardon, and he puffed hard on a cigarette. Holt held a palm toward Jardon's face.

25

"The cook," said Holt.

"What about him?"

"Remember him mentioning a foot?"

"A what?"

"A foot," said Holt. He picked up a leg and slapped the bottom of his shoe.

"When?"

"At the Jeep," said Holt. "At the restaurant."

"Why the fuck would he mention a foot?"

"Ha," Holt yelled and looked at Jardon.

"But he said," said Jardon, blowing smoke. "He said he'd hold up a thumb. He said if it was okay. Thumbs up."

"If what was okay?"

Holt glanced over both shoulders. A girl with large breasts walked near, but he shooed her away. Holt looked at Jardon. He looked at Trotter. He looked at Jardon again. "Show him," he said.

"Show me what?"

Jardon nodded his head and dropped his cigarette into an empty beer bottle. He reached into his backpack and took out a large jar. He set it on the table. Thud. Trotter moved his face toward it. He looked at Jardon. He looked back at the jar. A foot spinning on an axis in thick liquid, toes pointing down. It looked like an exhibit.

This is what Jardon knew:

"Javi was born right here in this building to a prostitute mother and he lived here until he was twelve," Jardon pulled a fresh cigarette from a pack and lit it and heaved smoke toward Trotter and Holt, who fanned the smoke from their faces. "Out there, in the cage, that's not a monkey," he said and took another drag. "That's a boy in a suit. If we hang around here long enough, if what Javi told me is true, that monkey comes inside and sits on a table and a whore gives its rubber penis a blowjob," Jardon ashed into an empty bottle. "Javi used to dress up as the monkey."

"You're fucking kidding me," said Trotter, and he tapped the glass of the jar.

"No," said Jardon, "but he was smart," Jardon nodded at them both. "He used to walk around finding change on the floor in the mornings and he'd take that money and go into town and he'd buy gum and sell it to the drunk tourists on the road for profit and he saved up money to go to college."

"He paid for college with gum money?" said Holt.

"Yeah," said Jardon, thumbing the filter of his cigarette. "That and wrestling," he said. "He was a luchador. They called him Nino del Oro."

"How the hell does that get us here," Trotter asked. He took the foot off the table and handed it to Jardon.

Jardon took the foot in one hand. "There's some stuff missing," Jardon said, cradling the foot. "I know he didn't graduate college. I know he's got a wife and kids somewheres in Mexico he sends money to, and I know he's diabetic," he held the jar to his face. "That's why they took his foot. He had to miss a couple days of work."

Holt slapped his hand to the table. "He got a foot cut off and only missed a couple days?"

Jardon juggled the foot to his other hand. "Maybe a few," said Jardon.

"Why we got it here now?"

Jardon nodded. "Javi can't come back across," he said. "He's illegal. They'd keep him. But he aims to have his whole body buried here eventually."

"Piece by piece?"

Jardon smiled a smoky smile. "No I think the whole thing, once he finally goes. But I guess he wanted to start with this," Jardon lifted the foot toward Holt.

"What now?" Holt asked.

Jardon leaned toward the table and ashed toward the ground. "Out that door is a courtyard," he said pointing with his cigarette, "with a fountain that doesn't work, and in the corner of the courtyard there are a couple banana trees, and we're supposed to bury the foot in the front of those trees in the courtyard."

"Just bury it? No prayer?" Holt and Trotter laughed.

"He said if we could, to get some mariachis to play while we were digging the hole, but he said it wasn't necessary that it'd just be a nice touch."

"Any particular song?"

Jardon thought for a minute. He dropped his cigarette into a beer bottle. "Nah, I don't think he said."

Trotter teethed his cleft. "I think I need more absinthe."

"What do you think?" asked Jardon. "Bartender seems nice enough. How bout we just ask him?"

"No," said Holt. He tapped the glass. "No need to make this weirder than it is."

They watched for girls. They watched the tender.

"Alright," said Holt. "When I say, go."

Everyone was turned, every back to them. "Go."

Trotter went first, ducking his feet chewing the dust as he flew through the door. Holt walked smooth. Jardon walked backwards whistling.

In the middle of the courtyard a dirt-filled fountain, the ground covered with weeds, and high above a full moon. In the corners banana trees. In every corner banana trees.

"Didn't say which one, did he?" Holt said.

"No," said Jardon, and they walked to the far corner.

"What do we dig with?" asked Trotter. Holt held up his hands.

The three, on hands and knees, moving dirt with their fingers, scraping the loose soil into piles frantic and fast as they could. A noise. A whore and a man, standing in the door way. Digging stopped. The two figures kissed.

Jardon whispered, "It's the old man."

The old man pulled away from his whore. He looked toward the far corner.

"Boys," he said, and he lifted his cane, he made to come near them, they didn't want him to see. Trotter made a noise like puking. Then they all made noise like puking. Fake puking and digging, "I wouldn't come over." Fake puking then digging the moon over head, furiously moving. Fake puking then digging. Then the old man laughed, "It really is your first time."

The bartender looked at their hands. "What have you been doing?"

"Nothing," said Holt. Jardon looked around the room. Trotter dragged his teeth across his cleft.

"Either way," said the bartender, "I don't think you should have more of that stuff. Stick to something more normal."

"Fine," said Holt. He ordered a round of tequila shots with beer chasers. The three leaned against the bar and drank. Then they drank some more. Then they danced with whores, then they drank. Then dancing. Then drinking. And toasting Javi and dancing.

The cabby dropped them at the Jeep and they stumbled to it.

"I don't think I can drive," said Holt.

"No," said Trotter. "No driving. We'll sleep in the Jeep."

"It rhymed," said Jardon, and he picked at the needles on his tongue.

The three laughed and climbed in. They locked their doors. They closed their eyes.

In the dark something stirred. It had been hours. Trotter opened his eyes. Men in suits, their tired faces heaving, walked single file down an otherwise empty road. Trotter watched them for a moment. They were moving toward the bridge. One of them looked at Trotter. Looked at him hard, the two locking eyes. The man shook his head. He straightened his tie, clicked his shoes and nodded. Trotter smiled at him. Then the man smiled back. Trotter buckled his seatbelt and went back to sleep.

FAKE PREGNANT

I

The only reason I know anything about that weekend at all is because Jesse was fake-pregnant and not drinking, and so she stayed coherent long after we left the commercial-director's hotel room. He was a weird little islander type, with coconut-husk hued skin and hair the length of a modest woman's. I don't remember him leaving his bed. He sprawled there with limbs in every conceivable direction and his head propped on a pillow. I dribbled a tennis ball against the marble tile and he stared at a shirtless boy who asked me to stop. I pocketed the ball and asked if we could get room service and Jesse told me I was rude, but she had to say it twice because the music came grumbling in beefy from the other room and I couldn't hear her the first time. "No," said the director. "It's not rude at all." Then he patted his belly and looked at the shirtless boy who disappeared for a minute or so. Then the director asked Jesse to sit on the bed's edge beside him so he could, "Stroke her hair." Which she did. Guardedly. "I could put you in commercials," said the director. Then the shirtless boy returned ferrying a small tray that cradled some manner of pink cocktail in a martini glass and a bottle of champagne aside two empty flutes. The shirtless fella served the director first before pouring me a glass of champagne, then he waltzed toward Jesse, who, with a palm opened toward him, declined to drink. "Darling you must, it's Cristal," the director said. "She can't," I said. "She's pregnant." The director lifted his head from the pillow. "I'm only fake pregnant," said Jesse. "Her fiancée's dancing in the other room," I told the director. "I see," said the director. "How delicious."

II

"Do you remember the horse ride?" "No." "Do you remember the circus midget?" "No." "Do you remember the boat captain named Jacque who promised to sail you from Miami to Cancun in three days time any time you were ever in South Florida so long as you gave him a week's notice?" "No." "I think he gave you his number." "Really?" "Check your pockets." "Holy shit. Captain Jacque Stern." "Do you remember the tennis ball, and how the shirtless kiddo stripped it from you?"

III

Vague whispers of teensy nipples, stiff as hard candy against my cheek as I wrestled his light body to the ground, and his skin, smooth as a shark's, slipped across my face and his nails clawed my neck, and the director, laughter like helium hissing across the open sphincter of a balloon, "Get my camera," and then the tennis ball gone, and then the shirtless boy off me.

IV

"How long was that before we left the hotel?" "It was after we left the hotel." "I think we were on marble. My knees are sore." "Cement." "Where?"

"Top floor of the parking garage where Monte keeps his balloon." "Monte?" "The director." "Balloon?" "Yes. Hot air. You rode in it. You puked down on the city and kept singing the balloon, the balloon, the balloon is on fire we don't need no water let the mother fucker burn." "Was the shirtless fellow with us?" "No you wouldn't let him on. You actually tried to keep Monte from coming aboard, but he was the only one who knew how to fly it." "And your fiancée?" "You'd gotten rid of him hours before." "How?" "You told him the baby was yours." "How did he take it?" "I think it would have been better if he didn't think you were my brother."

V

But the bad thing is that Jesse got real pregnant by the commercial director, and the kid came out with a kangaroo arm, and we saw her ex-fiancée in line at a Ferris wheel about six years later. Me, Jesse and the gimp kid. The fiancée was with a new woman. He leaned into her and whispered something in her ear. Jesse started crying. She knew he said something bad.

WHISPER TO SCAR

The boy thinks I've stolen his hand. He thinks I've hidden it. Locked it away in a cupboard. That's what I do with the food. I lock it away so that he can't find it. If I didn't he'd eat everything. Then he'd get fat. Fatter than he is. Thirteen years old and three hundred pounds. Pale thick fat slapped around him, as if God was making a snowman, but used fat for snow.

He's got a bad smell. Nothing keeps him clean. His body rejects itself, sending beads of sweat racing out pores as he sits. He's a slimy bubble of lard, with the heavy-pepper reek of an obesity from mayonnaise. I wish he weren't my son.

At the moment he's staring at the place where his hand used to be. Before it got infected and had to be removed. It's a gentle lobe, but more than rumor of incident. It looks like a hotdog end, sown up into itself.

I've caught him talking to it. Whispers.

"Come back out," he once murmured into the folds.

But it won't come back out. I've told him it's gone.

"Where'd you put it?" he'll ask.

"I didn't put it anywhere," I tell him. "It's just gone."

I never tell him true. That I had the doctors pitch it. They said I could keep it. My guess is they'd have put it in a jar. Sent it home in a paper bag so people couldn't see it. Can you imagine? Walking through the hospital with a hand floating in liquid. Children crying. Weak-stomached patients puking on the linoleum.

The thing rotted. The boy was with his mother. He mangled his fingers on a tin can of soup. Cream of asparagus. He got into the pantry when she wasn't looking. He opened up the can and ate it with his fingers. Cold. Congealed. His hand must've been too big to reach the bottom. Instead of getting a spoon he just forced it. Mashing his fingers against the tin cylinder, clawing at the last remnants of green soup on the bottom. I can only imagine how he bled. His blood probably filled the container, and I've a hunch he ate that too. Drank it from the can. Making those pig sounds. Those grunts. Giving his approval.

"So good," he says when eating. "So good."

No matter what he's eating he always says it. Could be raw potato. Could be cottage cheese. He doesn't know the difference.

His mother didn't find him for hours. She was probably out with her boyfriend. Huffing paint. Snorting meth. Videotaping sex in some basement. She's like that. A small town fiend. Shoulders that scrape up through her flesh. Gums receding. Pimples. Tattoos. Stringy unwashed hair and cigarette breath. This was back when things were good for her. This was back when she was still a waitress at the Waffle House.

We've been separated for seven years, and she blames me. Says it's my fault to my face. I remind her why we got divorced, and that always kills her.

"It was an accident."

That's her defense.

When he was younger she was pushing Timmy on a swing. He bounced from the saddle and landed on his head. Skull busted open into the gravel. I guess she scooped some gravel up into the bust and it must've mixed his wiring, changed his mechanics, because he used to be normal before the accident.

At the moment he's sitting Indian style on the floor, the fat from his abdomen spilling over his trunk-thick legs, smelling like hot-peppery-mayonnaise and whispering at the scars where his hand used to be.

His mother's in minimum security. The reason? Neglect. I still don't know where she was when it happened. I've asked her. She won't tell me.

But that's not the worst part. The worst part is that she didn't clean it. Just wrapped it up in gauze. Some days later, when he came home to me, I picked off the crusted bandage and a stench like garbage disposal filled my face. I dry heaved.

In court she said she tried to clean the wound but the boy wouldn't let her.

"He's strong," she told the jury, "he wouldn't let me at it."

"Did you notify anybody who could help?" the district attorney asked.

"To be honest," she said, "I didn't even think about that."

She got eighteen months and lost split-custody privileges. The jury was probably lenient on her because of Timmy's condition. It's not like the boy was ever going to do anything terribly productive with his hand. But that was her fault too. No matter what it is she got them to think.

Timmy sometimes asks about his mother. He's always asking for something. Food. Mommy. His hand.

I tell him she's away. I don't know if he understands or not.

My girlfriend Jennice thinks I should take more time explaining it to him. But what good would that do?

Jennice has a messed up kid too. A daughter called Kendra. She's blind, deaf and paralyzed. Sometimes she makes noise. Sometimes she drools.

Every now and then she smiles. That's kind of adorable.

Jennice is probably a better looking woman than I could normally get. I met her at a function for Timmy's school. Her husband left her shortly after Kendra was born. Most of us at the function were single.

Jennice has blonde hair and a smooth face. She has a beautiful body, and she's real good in bed. She makes noises. She likes to move around.

But sometimes the noises she makes remind me of Kendra. The way she moans. Then I start thinking about the drooling. While having sex. It's distracting. It makes me sick. It makes me wonder if there's something wrong with me, because I don't like thinking about Kendra. At least not that way. But the thoughts just kind of whisper around my head. They're attached to the noises.

I doubt Jennice and I will be together too long. It's not just the Kendra thing. There's other issues. For one Jennice is always questioning how I raise Timmy. I don't question how she raises Kendra. She's always trying to get me to do all kinds of things with him and to spend more time explaining things. She thinks I should send him away to a camp every summer where he can be with other kids like him.

"They'll teach him to work," she tells me, "how to function on his own."

I can't see how they could teach him much. I can't even get him to quit talking to his scar. And besides I don't tell Jennice how to raise her child. All she does is sing to Kendra, and wheel her around and towel her drool. And yet, somehow, she's the better parent.

One of the guys at the garage where I work has a boy Timmy's age. The two boys were even friends before the swing-set thing. His kiddo plays basketball and baseball and football. He's always going to games and telling me stories. He's always showing me trophies and photos of the kid in his uniforms. I think he does it just to piss me off. Bragging to me about what his kid can do. Reminding me what Timmy can't.

Two years back I bought a fishing boat. Nothing too special. Just a ten foot all-weld. Fifteen horsepower out-board motor. Just something good enough to go out and spend time alone in. Go out. Drop line. Catch fish. But I haven't gotten many chances to take it out since the boy's mother was put in jail. Nobody takes him for the weekends anymore. It's hard to find a sitter that will watch him.

One day Jennice told me that I should take Timmy. That it's something he would enjoy. She must have argued the point well, because I took him along.

We woke up early and packed an ice box. We motored out past the flats to fish the edge of the canal. It was early. It was calm. I don't even think the shrimpers were out.

Timmy asked his scar if it liked to fish. He was sitting with his legs dangling over the side of the boat, his feet breaking the surface of the water. The weight of his body was a strain on the ballast. The boat dipped where he sat. I had just casted a bait shrimp out into the laguna. We were right on the ridge. Beneath us the bottom sank from three to twelve feet. I could stand off the back of the boat. But in front, where Timmy sat, was above head.

I thought about how easy it would be. Like an accident. Him falling into the water, then splashing around in circles as his left hand pulled across the surface and his nub pierced through clean.

I reeled up the slack in my line. I set my pole in a holster.

"Hey, Timmy," I said.

"Yes, Daddy."

"That life jacket don't look too comfortabl you," I said. "Why don't you hand it here."

"Ah, sure thing, Daddy," he said. "Sure thing."

So with his one good hand he unlatched the jacket. It was a struggle for him, but he got it off. Then he handed it to me real slow and went back to staring at his scar.

"Hey, Timmy," I said.

"Yes, Daddy?"

"I think I know where your hand is."

He got excited, and I breathed heavy. My heart was crazy in my chest. Small waves lapped the side of the boat. Birds called out as they worked the shallow water behind us.

The boy started slapping his one hand against his nub. I guess trying to clap. The motion rocked the boat. Up and down. And Timmy kicked his feet in the water.

"Oh where is it, Daddy?" he asked. "Where's my hand?"

Then I was quiet. I swallowed. It was hard.

I took a stick of gum from my front shirt pocket. I placed it in my mouth and chewed.

Timmy watched all of this quietly, his face grinning.

"Look over the boat," I said, and Timmy stared over the bow down into the dark green water. "It's down there," I told him. "It's in the water."

"I don't see it," he called out. "I don't see it."

"Oh, it's down there," I told him, "you've got to get closer." I blew a bubble and pointed with my finger.

Timmy put his face down toward the water. He was hunched low over the side of the boat. I could see his reflection. He was smiling big.

He moved in closer. The boat sagged. His hands were on the edge. He was rocking gently. And then, just as he was about to take the plunge, his muscles tense against the metal frame as if to push his body forward, my line whistled out, screaming into the distance as some unseen fish took the hook with my fresh-cast shrimp and went running.

I grabbed the pole. I pulled back in one swift motion. The rod arced like a rainbow. It was a big fish. I could tell by the drag. Then I was standing. And Timmy was standing too. His body right next to me. Nestled against my arm. Large and soft. His stub on my shoulder. His eyes on the line. And as I fought the fish he kept on screaming, "Daddy, you caught my hand. Oh, Daddy, Daddy, you caught my hand."

SHORT BUS

Pappi likes to pop-lock, which is funny to watch because he's retarded and he's got no neck. He likes to dance, and he likes rap music. That morning he held his fingers out as though barrels of guns. He wagged his thumbs like crashing hammers. He did this in time with the beats blasting from the speakers. He wiggled his body and it looked like an off center gumdrop ready to fall. Everybody loves him. No one wanted to see him hurt. I gave him the first bulletproof vest and made sure it fit snug. We shook hands. His is calloused and I have no idea why. I've been padding his grades all year. The fat little bastard doesn't do shit.

Pappi threw his arm around his girlfriend Lidia. She's retarded too. They kissed and it looked disgusting. It sounded even worse. But I let it go because I knew it was love.

"Who wants cupcakes?" I asked, and a roar of excitement piled up from their throats.

This is how I got them ready. Sugar, soda pop and gangsta rap.

Pappi smashed blue icing into his lady-friend's face. I poured three-liters like they were Dom Perignon. A boom box screamed fuck, nigger, shit, bitch. . . and then one of my other kids screamed hooray. Then they all screamed hooray. HOORAY! HOORAY! HOORAY! HOORAY!

The short bus waited outside. I thought they'd never know what hit them.

"Men are going to get killed here today," I said

to Manuel which is funny because he doesn't know English. "And I'm going to kill them."

Manuel just talked to his palm in a language only he understands, but my assistant gave me a high five and said, "Tom Cruise is the shit."

"Kevin Costner," I told him. "It's from *Open Range.*"

"Same difference," he said, and it's funny because he's Mexican and they think all white people look the same.

"You really think we'll have to do some shooting?" he asked as he slammed a clip in a gun.

"Not if we play it right," I told him. "Not if we're smart."

You might be wondering why they gave me this job? Even though I picked my nose during the interview? Even though I burped and scratched my balls? Even though I sat there thinking, *Please don't hire me, please don't hire me, please don't hire me?*

First, there were two women on the interview panel and they were probably trying to save me. Second, there was a bald guy there who must have thought I looked cool because he gave me a fist bump when I walked in the room. Third, I had a college degree, and, according to my probation officer, that was all they were looking for. Fourth, perhaps the most important reason:

The interview was held in the same classroom where I would teach. The lights were dim. The air was cold. The space felt nervous.

"Have you always wanted to be a teacher?" the fatter woman asked me once the interview was underway.

"Of course not," I told her.

"Really. What did you used to want to be?"

"Hard to say." I thought about it while they rustled papers. "Probably a fireman."

The bald man's shirt wasn't tucked in. He smiled and said, "But you want to be a teacher now?"

I smiled back. "That's kind of why I'm interviewing," I told him.

Then the prettier woman cleared her throat, "And why do you want to be a teacher now?" she asked me.

"To help the kids," I said and smiled.

And that, or so I'm told, was the best answer any of the interviewees gave.

They said *congratulations*. I was a Special Ed teacher.

I thought back to my own high school. I thought about the special kids there and how we saw them when they sold tacos and when they'd go to PE with their gym shorts pulled over their jeans. They were clumsy. Some of them would grunt like pigs as they walked through the halls. They looked allergic to milk. Or like undercooked versions of actual people. Most of them had regular relatives, and so you'd know their names and you'd say hello when you saw them in the halls. They smiled when you spoke with them, especially if they remembered you.

Once, for a joke, I put a note in a taco one of them was selling. The note said, "Save us." I thought it was hysterical. I stopped this Down syndrome kid named Joey. He was carrying a basket. I slid the note in a taco and wrapped it back up in foil. Joey just watched me. His mouth open. I could taste his breath.

"What," he said, "are," he said "you doing?" His eyes didn't line up, and his cheeks jiggled like raw oysters.

"I'm a soldier in the war on drugs," I told him.
"What?"
"You've never heard about Nancy Reagan?"
"What?"

"The first lady."

"First?"

"Hurry up," I told him. "And don't tell anyone you saw me."

Then the kid stumbled down the hall with his basket of tacos, and I laughed as he waddled and waved when he looked over his shoulder.

He sold the taco to a Christian girl who wore a chastity ring. She was the prettiest girl in our school. She looked like a Barbie doll that hadn't grown up yet. She had long blonde hair, green eyes and the perkiest body. She acted insane with her religion and she wanted to be a savior like Jesus, and she told everyone about the note in the taco and how it must mean that the kids were being taken advantage of. She made it sound like they were slaves. Everyone believed her because of the way she looked and because of the ring she wore, and after a while all her friends boycotted the tacos. They even passed out little flyers that said, "Say No to Tacos." They got lots of attention. The newspaper even did a story on it. Mr. Blake, the Special Ed teacher, was quoted as saying, "My kids can't even read and write. They can't pass out notes. Maybe it's you who's retarded." Then there was talk because Mr. Blake seemed nasty, and they fired him, and the kids quit selling tacos.

Later that year someone walked in on the chastity-ring girl getting ass fucked in the upstairs bedroom of some rich kid's house. I think it was at a party, but I don't remember all the details. After that we all called her Poop Shoot Princess, but she kept on wearing her chastity ring, though I'm not really sure she deserved to.

Here's what happened on my first day teaching: The only things I took with me were raw eggs and tortillas. I parked as close to the exit of the parking lot as I could. A white-bearded man leaned against a white Ford pickup smoking a cigarette. He called over to me, "You the new guy?" and smoke poured from his mouth. The door of his truck was open and Lynyrd Skynyrd was playing on the radio.

"Sure am," I said, half grinning with nerves.

"You'll probably need some of this." He handed me a leather sided flask.

I shrugged my shoulders, ducked my head into the cabin of his truck and took a quick sip. It was Amaretto. I was expecting something harder.

"Takes the edge off," he said.

"Thanks," I told him. My mouth tasted like sugar.

"You working with the gimps?" he asked.

"What?" I didn't know how to answer.

"The retards, the specials," he said, and flicked his cigarette away. It bounced off the asphalt and the cherry busted and embers flew in every direction.

"I guess."

He laughed a sort of big hipped laughter and slapped my shoulder and said, "You poor son of a bitch."

I took another sip of the amaretto and handed the flask back to him. "Thanks," I said. Then I headed into the building.

I was hired after the school year had begun. The kids had chased off their other teacher. They don't tell you these things until after you've signed your contract, until after you've filed for your emergency certificate, until after you've passed your test.

I met with the pretty woman from my interview in the office. Her name was Hillary. She told me my schedule while we walked through the halls. When we were outside my classroom she asked if I had any questions.

"Just one," I said. "What did they do?"

"Excuse me?" She looked puzzled.

"The kids," I said.

"Oh," she said.

"To run off the other teacher?"

"Yes," she scratched her head and looked down the hall. She had a soft face and a gentle slouch at the shoulders. She seemed warm and smelled like syrup and I wanted to touch her. To put my cheek against her sweater. To tickle the crook of her knee with my tongue. To lie in repose beneath the bridge of her glasses. "They tried to stab her with scissors."

"Excuse me?"

"Scissors," she said, and moved her hand in a stabbing motion.

"Which one?" I asked.

"Which one what?"

"Which one tried to stab her?" I asked. I wanted to know who to look out for.

"All of them," she told me.

"All of them?"

"Well not Marisol," Hillary said. "She can't really move."

Then Hillary motioned for me to go inside. The room reeked. An unnatural mixture of antiseptic and bad breath. It was cold. It was bright. The fluorescents above flickered a frigid stillness down. There were kids everywhere. A small and angry brood of them. Their befuddled faces staring at the doorway like a pack of bunged up thumbs.

"Their bus got here early today," said Hillary. She smiled and I wanted to tap her teeth with my fingernail. To trip and land longways on her tongue tip. To listen for the ocean in her bellybutton. "They haven't had breakfast yet," she said.

Let me tell you about the kids:

Manuel spends the day walking in circles and slapping his classmates on the ass. When he's not doing that he flips off the light switch. We call out his name and he laughs. He doesn't speak anything, I think I already told you, but he likes to whisper some odd phrase into is palm while he walks around. It sounds like this, "Osh, osh, osh-ack-aba." He always wears the same thing. A grey hooded sweatshirt and black jeans. I think he has a T-shirt beneath the sweatshirt, but I don't know because I've never seen. We've tried to wash it several times but he spits and scratches when we touch the zipper. He walks around chewing the sleeves and slobber soaks the fabric, and so it smells like a month's worth of morning drool caught in a bucket. He looks undead. Like a monster ate his insides and wears his skin for a suit. Or like a scarecrow that is somehow alive.

I told you about Pappi and how he likes to dance. I told you about Lidia and how she's Pappi's girlfriend. But what I didn't tell you is that they look almost identical. They both have Down syndrome and they're both good and rotund. The main difference between them is that Lidia has long hair and Pappi's head is near-clean shaven. Plus Pappi wears glasses and Lidia always carries a magazine. She rustles the pages. She likes the way they sound.

I haven't even mentioned Jesús, which is funny because he's my smartest kid. He talks all day long. He likes to come up and put his hand on my shoulder.

"Maybe you could help me get on the wrestling team," he told me the first time I met him.

"I'll check," I said.

"You do that," he went on. He was nodding his head and his whole body went with it. He looked almost ready to break into dance and he was ropy and rapid and restless and his eyes looked alight as though fuses were chasing back toward a coming explosion in his brain. "I won't let you down," he told me. "I could whip my weight in wildcats."

Jesús also wears glasses. He likes country

music. I know that because of his clothes. He wears tight Wrangler denims and weird-colored button-ups and black leather boots and he has a large silver belt buckle.

Once he told me he needed to get Nyquil for his mom so she could come down. He told me he needed to get Freon and a hula hoop so that she could be a ballerina.

"Do you know what a ballerina is?" he asked me.

"A dancer," I told him.

"That's right," he said. "A dancer." And he bobbed in that way of his. "My mom's a queen." He ran the back of his hand across his mouth and flipped his attention at something I couldn't see. "But I need to get her some Nyquil with a stick on it so she could float up like a ballerina with a hula hoop on, and I could put the Freon on the hula hoop, and then she could come down. Every single day," he said. "Every single day."

None of it made sense. But did it explain a lot?

The only other kid was Marisol. Something about her was magic. She didn't do anything but stare. She could barely move on her own, and when she did it wasn't voluntary. But everyone talked to her. Told her their whispers. It was safe. Your secrets died in her brain. She smelled like lavender and there was some invisible and silent music that swam around her, and it was the smell and the music that made your mouth to talk and your eyes to go quietly inward as though heavied by honey or wrapped up in steam.

Everything I know about the kids I learned the first day. They don't hide anything. Their minds can't grasp shame.

My assistant's almost the same way. He's a huge fellow. He thinks he's a Mexican but he must be part Indian. You can picture him hunting buffalo barefoot on the plains, naked except for bits of leather and carrying a weapon made from a stick and a stone. He's got broad shoulders and a face as flat as the blade of a shovel. His hands are huge. It looks like he has extra fingers. He asked me to call him Rocky, though his name's really Rick.

Rocky's been working at this school for five years. Before that he was a professional rugby player, but he had a bad accident and had to give it up. He took a shoulder to the leg, and his knee cap popped from its ligament and rolled up toward his thigh.

"It burned like hell," he told me. "Like someone opened my leg and packed it with hot coals."

"What'd you do?"

"I threw up."

"In front of everyone?"

"Everyone," he said.

He says there wasn't much money in the sport. He says there wasn't much fame.

"Why'd you do it," I asked him.

"Just loved the game."

"And this job?"

"It's okay," he said. "It's easy."

He smiled when Hillary introduced us. He told me he would help me in any way that he could.

"Good," I told him. "Throw away all the scissors."

The first day was hell. I chased Manuel in circles. I pulled Pappi and Lidia apart. Jesús kept telling me stories about his mother. He showed me the pictures in his wallet at least a dozen times.

I tried to teach them how to make tacos in the kitchenette in the room but Pappi farted during the lesson and everyone laughed. My assistant even laughed. Like it was the funniest thing ever. So I trashed the idea, and the tacos, and I sat in a chair. I stared at them. I could tell they were bored. Jesús kept looking around the room. I think he was looking for something to stab me with.

During my conference period I walked to the teacher's lounge. I sat by myself at a table and watched. I thought about the teachers from the high school I went to. It occurred to me these people were just different versions of them. I knew what subjects they taught just by looking. The math teachers had polyester shirts and the coaches wore jerseys and the science teachers were tight wound and the English teachers looked like cigar ashes. It was scary.

Then I went to see Marisol. She was fragile too and had to be kept apart in this other room. The nurse assigned to her smiled when I came by, and she asked if I'd watch Mari while she ran an errand.

"Sure," I told her. "What do I need to do?"

"Nothing," she said.

I sat on a chair and watched Mari breathing. The radio was on playing classical music. Marisol's body lay crooked. Her limbs shaped like a crab's and pulled tight toward her. She had cropped brown hair and a cleft lip. She had a wide smashed nose and raw almond colored skin. That was the first time I talked. Maybe it was the smell. Maybe it was the music. I whispered how I never wanted to be a teacher and all about probation and my DWI and about the taco note and how it got the teacher fired and about every stick of gum I'd ever stolen and every drink of liquor that I'd ever let steal my brains. All of the girls I'd slept with. Every fight I'd been in. I spread out as I spoke, my fibers seemed loosened. And when the bell rang and the nurse came back and my conference was over, the steps seemed serene moving back toward my room.

At the end of the day we took the kids outside and waited for the bus. It was sunny out. The kids were spastic. I broke a sweat trying to keep them all in one place. They kept trying to get away from me. Up and down the sidewalk. Round and round the

50

tree. Then the short bus swung around the corner, low to the ground, smelling sweet and metallic from diesel. Rocky and I led the kids to the bus. Mari was loaded by a lift on the back. The rest of the kids gawked aboard and I introduced myself to the driver.

"Hey, chief," he said. He wore a white ball cap that said NASCAR.

Then Rocky climbed on the bus, and the driver asked if I was coming.

"Where?"

"Gonna drop off the kids and head to the bar," he said.

"In a short bus?" I asked.

"Why not?"

I didn't have an argument, so I climbed on.

The short bus hissed hypnotic. All the kids fell asleep. I sat on a fake leather seat that stuck to the skin of my arm. We rolled along with windows open. A half hour passed, getting them home. They either lived in chipped-paint apartments or in houses with weedy lawns. Rocky screamed a grito when the last kid got off.

The bar we went to seemed made in simpler days. It rested on the edge of a canal. The jukebox was filled with singers from Mexico that I didn't know. We drank tequila from a bottle that a waiter placed on the table. We had shot glasses and small bowls filled with limes and salt. The tequila was hot and tasted like death, but the more you had of it the better it was. We all had a bit. It became pretty good.

"How'd your first day go, chief?" the driver asked me.

"Terrible," I said. But Rocky disagreed.

"It was a great day," he said. "No one tried to stab anyone."

"At all?" asked the driver.

"At all."

We sat for hours in the stale-simple air, swatting mosquitoes and me fake singing along with boleros. They knew all the words and laughed big at me. We got quicker at drinking. Each sip conditioned us, and as time drew on more and more customers showed, and our bottle emptied, and the two things seemed tethered, an inverse reaction, and once the bottle was drained, and the bar filled, they told me it was tradition for the new guy to pay, so I gave a wad of bills to a waitress on our way out the door. I don't remember getting back on the short bus, but I know they dropped me at my car in the parking lot and I drove home slowly.

I was starving. I went through my refrigerator once I got home. There was nothing to eat but Eggo waffles. I put them into the toaster and got out my Mrs. Butterworth's syrup. I twisted off the lid and the smell reminded me of Hillary. I kissed the small face on the side of the bottle. I imagined her wrapping me up in her tiny glass arms.

After I ate I stared at my phone. I knew no one would call it, and I had no one to call, but I wanted to hear voices, so I grabbed the phone book and flipped through it. I tried looking up Hillary, but her number wasn't listed. Then I looked through the Yellow Pages at the ads and the numbers. I had to hold one eye shut to read them. I came to a full page ad for the symphony. It reminded me of Marisol and the music in her room. I dialed the number. I got an answering machine. I don't really remember leaving a message.

As you might expect, the next morning I felt terrible, but I scraped myself out of bed and headed to work. I stopped at the store on the way. I bought more eggs and tortillas. The woman who wrung me up stared at my eyes.

"Rough night?" she asked.

"I think I'm still drunk."

I parked close to the school. I didn't feel like walking. I drove by the white-haired man smoking by his white truck. I waved. He laughed.

The kids were not early that day. Rocky and I cooked tacos before they showed up. He had a lopsided smile, and his hair was mashed to his skull.

We all ate together, except for Manuel. He just walked in circles and played with the lights. It was easier. Hillary stopped by. She stuck her head in the doorway and waved.

"Want a taco?" I asked.

"Oh," she said. She looked nauseous. "I'm not hungry but thanks."

Then Pappi farted and all of the kids laughed. I shrugged my shoulders. I was embarrassed. Hillary sort of smiled and walked off.

The best part of the day was my conference period. Rocky watched the kids and I left. I walked through the hallways and stared at the students. The boys looked younger than I did when I was their age. The girls looked older. After a while I got sick of walking. I went to sit in the room with Marisol. The nurse excused herself. The music was playing. I sat on a chair. I began whispering again. I told her about everything. My words melted around her. She rocked her head back and forth, her eyes closed like a fresh puppy searching out its mother for food. I told her about my father and how I hated him. I told her about my brother who had killed himself. I told her I missed him. How I held myself responsible. How I knew I could've been nicer, and my body hummed as I said it, and time fell from me like a damp towel, and that was how all my days went: I made sure the kids didn't stab each other, and I told my secrets to Marisol. Every day I felt good about everything. The weeks streaked by.

*   *   *

The symphony sent a cellist to play for Marisol. He showed up wearing a tuxedo and carrying a big black case. When I saw him coming down the hall I locked the door. I couldn't remember what I had left on the message.

"Sir," he said as he knocked. "I have come to play for you beautiful music."

I let him in. We shook hands and it was uncomfortable. He looked around. He cleared his throat.

"What you do is beautiful," he said. His thick Austrian accent sticky as cake. His hand shake was firm. His eyeballs were oily. "My sister was one of these," he said. Then he laid his hand level with an imaginary horizon and pulled his arm away from his body. It looked like a farmer scattering seed in slow motion.

He sat on a plastic chair in the middle of the room. He played Bach's Prelude in D minor. He introduced the piece and sank into his instrument. His fingers seemed so considerate of their movements. I dimmed the lights as he played, but the window blinds were open, and a ladder of light lay limp across Marisol's face. She drooled. Saliva slid from her cleft lips, and she pulled her hands to her chest, and she strained her neck forward, and she sniffed in every direction.

The cellist didn't see any of this. His eyes kept closed. He was distant in some way, somehow beneath the music. His cello smelt like a lit candle, and the scent carried on the notes. It poured through the air and pressed me against a wall, and Marisol and I breathed in time with the cellist, who breathed in time to the music, and the air seemed to hum like an electric appliance. Warmth filled me. Mesquite sap in the summer. And then we were all beneath the music, muted like a swimming-pool's light. I stood close enough to hear the hiss of the horse hair bow, the pulse of an animal better than me.

When he stopped my mouth filled with the flavor of chlorine. My purpose felt polished, and Marisol dozed mightily.Then the cellist wiped his instrument with a cotton cloth and put it back into the case.

"Thank you very much," I told him. "It was beautiful."

"It has been my pleasure," he said. "I had a beautiful audience."

We both looked at Marisol. Then I watched the cellist walk down the hallway and toward the exit.

Hillary's dating the coach of the debate team. At least that's what she told me when I asked her out.

"I can't," she said. "I'm involved."

"Oh, I just thought because you stop by and all."

"No, I'm sorry," she said. "You have the wrong impression."

"Obviously," I said.

Her boyfriend's name is Stafford. He teaches honors English. He has a red sports car and he knows tons of big words. At least that's how I imagined him in the seconds following my rejection. All Hillary told me was that he coached debate, but I've never met him, so I am not sure. Hillary came by the room to tell me about Marisol. The holidays were near. We had decorated. There was mistletoe hanging in the doorway above us.

"What about her?"

"She won't be coming back after Christmas."

"Why not?"

"Because she's been lying about where she lives."

"Mari can't lie," I said. I thought I was going to be sick on the floor.

"Well, her parents."

"But I've been on the bus," I said. "I've seen where she lives."

"From what I understand she just gets dropped off there, but she'd be graduating at the end of the year anyway so it's not that big of a deal."

"If it's not a big deal then why can't we fix it?" I said.

It was quiet. I felt like crying. I wanted to tear the mistletoe from the door. I wanted to burn it and use it to set other things on fire.

"It's the rules," Hillary said. "She lives out of district and she can't pay tuition."

"Tuition," I said. "This is a public school."

"Yes," she agreed, "but out of district parents can pay for students to attend."

"How much?" I said.

"I'm not sure," said Hillary. I could tell she wanted to leave. "You'd have to ask an administrator."

I didn't have the kind of money the administration needed. My heart ached when they told me. It must have been noticeable to everyone I saw.

"What's wrong, chief?" the bus driver said when I climbed on the bus.

"Just get me to the bar," I told him.

He drove fast. He was quick with his horn. We dodged through the lanes, and the kids jostled in their seats. We got them dropped off in fifteen minutes flat.

Marisol was our last drop off. I stepped off the bus and spoke to her mother. The mother looked like Mari but with straight legs and arms. She also had regular lips, and her hair was much longer. She told me she was sorry about having lied to the district. I told her that I didn't care and that I was going to try to help with the money. She grabbed both my hands and kissed them when I said it.

"The other school is terrible," she told me. "I don't want her to go there."

The tequila helped sooth me. My nerves were twisted and frayed and bleeding acid and caught on fire and tangled in a poisonous spider's web. We killed the bottle in total quiet. I looked at Rocky. He was wasted. He was rocking in his chair. His tolerance is shaky because of his being part Indian.

"S'wrong, boss?" Rocky asked.

"Mari," I said, and I realized I was wasted too because my words seemed to clang from me as though falling from an unmaintenanced machine, "changing schools," I continued, "unless we can get five grand." I sipped at my empty tequila cup, and the bus driver slammed his hand on the table.

"Why?" he said.

"Doesn't live where she says," I told him.

"I'd pick her up," he told us, "anywhere," he slammed his hand on the table again and the bottle fell to its side and began to roll off the table. "Anywhere," he barked again. Then he leaned into the center of the table and stopped the bottle with the palm of his hand, "I talk to her when I'm driving," he said. "I tell her my sins."

"Me too," said Rocky. And I was confused, and he saw the confusion wash over me and he shook his head and said, "Not while I'm driving. You know," he smiled and his eyes went empty. "She's the only one," he said and hiccupped, "knows I'm gay," he hiccupped again.

The bus driver and I looked at each other. We shook our heads. We shrugged our shoulders. We went blank in the face. We looked at Rocky. We looked at each other again and sort of nodded.

"What do we do?" the bus driver asked.

We sat. We thought. Silence. Every now and then a face would brighten, perhaps an idea, but nothing, the face would fade before anyone spoke.

Rocky's eyes were wondering across the room. He looked like a giant Indian princess. "I'm starving," he said. His words sounded like flowers.

"Me too," said the bus driver.

"There's good tacos down the way," said Rocky.

Then it hit me. Tacos. We'd sell tacos to get the money. Just like the kids at the high school I went to. I told Rocky and the bus driver. They thought it was brilliant.

"I'm going to need your help though," I told them. "I can't do it alone," I said. "It takes a village." My head felt like poison.

It took several weeks to file the proper paper work needed to have a fundraiser at school. We didn't have that kind of time. I called the mall and they said it was no problem for us to sell tacos there. We cooked. I brought in a pallet of eggs and a case of tortillas. I brought in a huge bag of potatoes and a huge bag of onions. I brought in a box of tomatoes the color of blood.

I had Lidia shred cheese. Manuel warmed tortillas. Pappi just sat on a chair bobbing his head. Jesús rolled the tacos. I wrapped them in foil. Rocky made the hot sauce, and cooked the potatoes and eggs. We loaded up baskets, like the kids from my high school, and we piled on the short bus and headed to the mall. We walked the halls like a gang of victims, hungry for hand outs and scaring the people. We got there early, before the stores opened. We were only allowed to sell to the mall employees. Most of them just looked at us and shook their heads no. They all wore brand new clothes. They all had razor sharp hairdos. We looked like the newspapers that puppies get trained on. When it was all done, when we had walked the mall hallways twice, when he had knocked on the doors, and rattled the cages, we tallied our money.

"Seven dollars," Rocky said.

"That's it?"

"Looks like it."

The baskets were full of cold potato and egg tacos. I was depressed. We sat on a bench.

"What now?" asked the short bus driver.

"I'm not sure," I told him.

Then I watched my kids. Pappi was dancing. There was music coming out of a shoe store behind us. Pappi was holding his hands like they were guns, and he drifted across the tile floor in a hurricane motion. There was a bank in the mall with a huge plate glass store front, and a teller inside was staring at Pappi. Then a guard came out and stood at the entrance. Pappi fake shot the guard with his fingers, and the guard put his hand to his chest and smiled and said, "You got me."

Then I whispered, "We'll rob a bank," so that only Rocky and the short bus driver could hear. "They'll never suspect it."

I thought it would be harder to convince Rocky. I knew the short bus driver would go along. He was old, and he had no family, and the only thing he did was drive the bus and get drunk.

Rocky shrugged his shoulders. "You gotta do what you gotta do," he said.

We formulated a plan. We knew we needed bulletproof vests and guns. We'd seen enough movies to know how it worked. I sold my car for five hundred dollars. We went to a gun show and bought our supplies. Rocky had to buy everything. My background was questionable.

We got vests for the kids and guns for the adults. The salesman at the gun show looked pleased with our purchase.

"Looks like a solid collection for in-home security," he said. He had wiry hair and his teeth overlapped.

The next morning we took the arsenal to school.

We loaded the bus once the kids finished their cupcakes. They're skin was electric. They had sugar-high blood. We chose a bank off of the expressway because it had a large parking lot we could get in and out of easily. The plan only worked if we made our escape. The bus jolted and bounced as it sped across the road.

This was our plan: We park the bus. We get the kids out. We go into the bank. We ask them for all of their money.

"Won't it take us a long time to get the kids back on the bus?" Rocky asked.

"Yeah but it's not like they'll be shooting at handicapped kids," I told him.

"And the getaway?"

"I'll handle that," the short bus driver said.

We told the kids it was a field trip. But Jesús was suspicious. "It sounds like stealing," he said.

"Do you want to be left on the bus?" I asked.

We pulled up to the bank. My hands were trembling. I stood at the front of the bus and looked at the children. A Christmas carol played on the bus driver's radio. My brother liked Christmas, and I thought about him. He was a good shot. I wished he was around, and I chambered a bullet.

"I say we go in blazing," said Rock, and his face went all rugby, something I'd never seen.

"No," I told him, "we've got to stay calm."

"Chief is right," said the driver. The transmission was in park and he must have feathered the accelerator because the engine gave a grumble.

"It's stealing," said Jesús, and I looked at

him and said, "You *will* stay on the bus if you say it again."

And then Rocky said, "Yeah," and his voice was a knot of rugby and it worried me.

"As long as we're calm enough in there everything should be okay, all we have to do is stick to the plan, we're going to go in and stand by the door, and then, Rocky. . ."

"I'm on it."

"Wait till I finish. . ."

"I'm waiting."

"Rock, you fire a shot into the ceiling. . ."

"Boom," he said.

"That's right," I said, "boom," and patted his shoulder, "and then after you fire the shot they'll all, I mean everyone in there, they'll all hit the ground and that's when I'll tell them why we came there, and then I'll explain that they're gonna be giving us the money, that they'll be placing it in the bags that I'll be giving to Pappi and Jesús, and. . ."

"I'm not doing anything," said Jesús. "I'm not stealing."

I looked him down. "I know it," I told him. "Do you want to know why?"

"Because it's wrong," he said.

"No," I told him. "It's because you'll be staying on the bus."

Then he slapped his hands against the back of the seat in front of him. "I don't like this field trip," he said, and his face fisted up like he was about to cry.

I looked at Rocky, "Where was I?" I asked.

"Pappi will be picking up money."

"That's right," I told him. "He'll pick it up in this bag." I pulled a black trash bag from out of my back pocket, and I held it up and thought about how heavy it'd be once it was stuffed with cash. "They'll load up this bad boy, and then we'll back out of there slow."

"Maybe fire a few more shots?"

"Not unless we have to," I said. "Not unless they fire first."

"I don't like this field trip," Jesús said again, and I shushed him and then said, "But yes, Rocky, if they start shooting we'll answer back." I lifted my gun and smiled at it and sort of marveled at how the black barrel was menacing and how I knew that it could get folks to give me their cash and how the cash could keep Marisol with me and that I could keep telling her my secrets and how all of the shame of the day would die as a story in her mind and how once it was out of me I'd be free of it. But then from nowhere Jesús screamed, "I don't like this field trip," and I don't know where the hell he got them but that sonoffabitch drove a pair of green-handled scissors down into my thigh so easily that it seemed like they belonged there, and my leg felt filled with heat and a stream of blood sprung up and Rocky barfed against his bus window and I accidentally shot the ceiling with my chambered bullet and Pappi started laughing and Lidia rustled the pages of a magazine and Manuel whispered to his palm and Mari didn't do anything and then a guard from the bank came out of the building and then the driver threw the bus in drive and hit the gas and we sped off with me screaming.

It took me over a month to heal. Hillary welcomed me back as I limped down the hall. "To be honest," she said. "We didn't expect you to return."

"Because of this," I said, and pointed to the spot where Jesús wounded me. "It'd take more than this to scare me away." I smiled at her. "Did you miss me?" I asked. And she reminded me about the debate coach, and I wanted to place my finger on her lips so she couldn't say anything. To run my fingers through her hair. To nibble the tips of her fingers.

I gimped down to my room and opened the door. The kids sat calmly in their seats and Rocky was wearing an apron. "Boss," he said as I made my way in, and then Jesús rocketed from his seat and ran up and put his head on my shoulder and told me how much he missed me, and he showed me the pictures in his wallet and then said, "I won't stab you again," and he nodded and rubbed his palms together. "I won't," he said, "I won't do it."

"I know you won't," I said and messed his hair. "Now," I said, "who wants to make tacos?" Then the whole classroom applauded.

Crazy

THE UNION OF SHERMAN AND GRANT

Sherman's first name was Tecumseh, really, after the Shawnee chief, but a priest tacked on William, after the Saint of Vercelli, on account of him needing a Christian name in order to be baptized, and it being the day of the Feast of Saint William. Grant's real first name was Hiram and his middle Ulysses. It was a clerical error when they enrolled him at West Point, and they wouldn't let him change back, so his middle name became his first and he somehow gained the initial S. It didn't stand for shit.

Sherman had been a job jumper, and Grant an alcoholic when the Civil War broke. They were kindred in their memories' miseries. They kind of seemed queer for each other. They hugged happily when they met. Sherman the older, sensitive to his general's feelings. It was the sensitivity that won the war. The Confederates were thumping the Union at Shiloh. Grant was wounded when Sherman went to advise retreat. *We've had the devil's day of it*, Sherman Said. *Lick 'em tomorrow though*, said the General. Sherman knew it'd destroy Grant to say the truth. He kept quiet. The next day the Union rallied. Killed nearly two thousand with their pummeling guns. The Union lost nearly the same number of men, but was dubbed victorious. Later the Confederate George Washington Cable wrote, "The South never smiled after Shiloh." It's imagined they embraced at that battle's finale. Their graying beards grazing as others carted away the dead.

FACE SO MILD

Hunt used to bust Jeff's ear raw with his fist. I saw him do it. I saw him bring that clenched thing down, sledging the lobe against his skull until blood made spray his face and shoulder blades. This was all some years back in high school. Incarnate Word—where the nuns hid their beyond-burgeoned bodies in loose-fitting habits, and their cheeks filled flush when their students muttered *fuck*. Hunt would strike him every day at lunch, but Jeff didn't mind it. He'd sit smirking on the lowest bleacher in the gymnasium, and I'd collect the dollar bills that folks would pay to see. Jeff couldn't feel much. He'd a name for the condition, but at last it escapes me. He could take most brutal aggressions in stride. You could kick him in the balls while he lit a cigarette smiling. "I felt it," he'd say exhaling smoke, "but it didn't faze me." We'd take in a killing on the show Monday through Thursday, and, come Friday, we'd skip out toward North Padre Island and catch the ferry to Port Aransas where we'd sip beers at the Sea Drift and look for trouble to come.

On those Friday afternoons Hunt and Jeff would run amok. Jeff didn't hold ills against Hunt for past bludgeonings, but after imbibing he'd find it funny to chuck fists against Hunt's shoulders and ribs, and they'd go to tussling, and once Jeff, who was broader than Hunt by some inches, pitched Hunt off the port side of the ferry toward Turtle Cove as we made our drunk way home, and we spent the night in Nueces County Jail in drenched clothes because Jeff had jumped in after Hunt, and I had jumped in after both of them, and we were soaked when the cops showed. We got cited with public intoxication and disorderly conduct, and some months later we worked off community service hours at Sea Side Cemetery digging and dirting the graves, and I've got a picture somewhere of me doing a handstand aside an open grave with Hunt and Jeff leaned against shovels on either side of me grinning.

Hunt and Jeff and I distanced after high school. Hunt's a millionaire's son and he went up to A&M College Station and studied business or marketing, and he went into real estate and I hear he makes a killing. I stayed at the A&M in town and studied art appreciation for three semesters before I realized I didn't appreciate much, and I dropped all my classes and got a job tending bar at a place downtown I'd rather not mention by name. Jeff got a job on a deep-sea boat grabbing fish for amateurs and clubbing sharks to death. It's one of those vomit-cruise catamarans, where thirty some odd tourists pay to be bobbed out deep, and they sit single file on either the port or starboard side facing the gulf with a short pole between their knees and a bowl of chopped mullet by their feet, and they drop their lines until they hit the floor, or until their bait gets gotten, and then they reel up whatever it is they've lucked into, but they're not allowed to unhook the fish, it's a liability, the boat's always tossing, there's fear they'd catch their fingers on the hooks, so they holler to Jeff, that's his job, he couldn't feel it if he set a hook to his bone, and he comes running down to pull off their snappers, or beat dead their sharks, and he hauls the fish aboard, holds them for the fishermen to see, and tags them and drops them in a well to be redistributed once the boat makes shore. It's not a romantic occupation, but he claims it pays well.

He says they make good tips, because they sell beer, and those who go out and catch both buzz and fish are prone to generosity. "The worst part of the job's not beating the sharks by a long shot," he told me. "That's fun," he said smiling. "The problem is seasickness is infectious. One of those fucks goes green and the whole tour turns. Thirty some odd losers loafing up on the decks. It stinks unimaginable. The dead bait and vomit and diesel fumes off the engines. You get back and have to hose everything down. The vomit and fallen bait collects like a raft being pushed toward the stern, and it clumps like some dirty dune, and splashes to the bay like a turd toward a toilet." He told me he could get me on a cruise if ever I wanted, but I can't take him up on the offer.

Recently I've been watching a lot of videos. I'm not sure what's into me. I've had internet in my house for years, but recently I've been looking at things. Things maybe I shouldn't mention. I've liked girls all my life, but I've always been shy on them. I didn't take a date to prom even. I just went by myself real casual, though there were girls who would've gone with me, had only I asked. I'm not much in conversation with them, but I do like their form. Sometimes I'll wear my sunglasses to the shopping mall, and I'll watch them as I'm passing, because they can't see my eyes. I like when they slide the clothes hangers as they're browsing or when they sip soda through straws. There's a lady at work I'll have drinks with on Sundays when we close early, but there's a difference with her because I'm not sure she likes men. But lately the videos have been different. Not women, not girls. Not sex or sexual nature.

I found this site that shows fist fights. It's all videos that high school kids take on their cell phones. They're never high quality, and most aren't even a minute long. Sometimes they're on trampolines, and sometimes they're in bathroom stalls, and sometimes they're in fields of grass, and there's one that's in a gym. It's only twenty seconds. I watch it when I'm able. A lanky kid walks up to a broad shouldered fella real casual and sends a fist to his face. The punched kid just takes it. His face so mild. It's as though he's receiving a blessing. I wonder if he has the same condition Jeff does? I wonder if he feels a thing?

Sometimes for no reason I'll drive over to North Padre and catch the ferry back and forth and stand at the spot along the guard rail where we all three went over, and I'll sort of smile there remembering. I miss a hunk of that time we had. Sometimes I even think about letting myself slip just to recreate it. Letting myself go face first down against the salt water. I know I could still do it, so long as someone went before me. But I was never much for leading. I was always scared of throwing a fist at the moment. I was always stuck worrying about how bad it would sting.

HOT MESS

My father used to ask at the dinner table if we needed water.

"Water?" he'd say and pass the rolls. "Ice water?" Then send the greens. "Cold water?" And the butter would go clockwise. "Need water?" Bread across the table.

My father set my brother's face on fire.

My brother's burnt face, his lips jagged and scarred, against my neck, parting as he laughs, and pressure as he pulls my hand behind me and drives my knuckles against my back. We're on the ground. His knees dig into my sides and my knees hit the hard floor below. Feet away the runners of my mother's rocker skate the tile in a pendulum course, crushing loose grout as she chuckles and phlegm breaks in her chest.

"What'll it be?" my brother asks.

Then my mother. "Y'all get along."

My cheek is against the cool tile. It's bruised, but that'll heal. My knees are scraped, but the scabs'll fall. My neck is warm from my brother's breath that draws from the melted nostrils sunk back toward his skull. It's a skull pocked with red mottled scars. Like bloody eggs left to dry in the pan.

My mother to me. "Go ahead say it."

"No."

Brother to me. "Say it."

"No."

My ears hiss. My knuckles are forced up my spine, and my arm's near breaking. My eyes are closed, but somehow wrapped in light. Then opened. Wide eyes in the dim living room where my mother spends her time hissing through her emphysema. I hear her spit towel flick my brother's back.

Mother to brother. "Let up on him."

Knuckles toward skull.

"Not till he talks."

My elbow burns every time I breathe. It's Sharp. Sharp. My legs tense. My feet flail. I can feel all my blood.

"Fine," I scream.

He lets my knuckles slip toward my toes. I breathe.

"Fine what?"

I stay silent. My brother drives my knuckles back toward my skull.

"Fine, fine, fine," I say my cheek slapping the tile. "I love my big brother."

My brother hacks a laugh, and my arm goes limp. Then his kiss. His mottled flesh against my face. My mother laughs, and her phlegm snaps. My body constricts when my brother presses against me to rise. Then the freedom from his weight.

"Good deal," my brother says. He walks into the kitchen and flips the light. "Let's eat."

My mother smoked three packs a day until the day of her diagnosis. In every old picture of her there's a cigarette between her lips, or she's reaching for an ashtray. She smoked so much that the walls in the house turned from yellow to green. So much my elementary teachers asked me if I smoked, because the stench followed me on my clothes wherever I'd go. In all my memories smoke pours from her smile. I used to think my mother made the clouds.

*   *   *

I'm in my father's old seat. My brother flips venison in a cast iron skillet. He forks the red meat and it whistles. His shirtless back is toward me, his broad shoulders pump as he turns the meat.

"It gonna be good," he says over his shoulder. He pulls the hot pan toward his hip and looks down in the steam.

"I don't like meat," I say.

My brother turns from the stove, moves wide stanced, his heels dropping against the tile. Pronounced and silly he pops his shoulders as he moves. Steam floats toward his face.

"You'll like this," he says reaching the table. His jeans sunk low. His hips like hide stretched antlers. He forks a piece hard. The prongs hit the pan. He holds the venison above my plate, brown and peppered, juices running the fork holes and hitting the plate in streaks. "Killed it myself."

"And if I don't?" I sip ice water.

My brother breathes deep through his fire-peeled nose. "You'd be back on the ground." He shakes the fork twice, and the venison falls.

The wall behind my brother's bed is covered with mounted animals. Fish and fowl and game. Centered above the headboard is a twelve-point buck with a gray tuft on his chin. We call the buck Charley. My brother's name is Abe.

This is not Charley between my teeth, salty and metallic, being torn slowly as my jaw constricts. That is barely Abe across the table, staring at a Zippo as he shovels meat between his scarred lips.

"New lighter?" I ask.

"It is," Abe says, and venison drops from his mouth to his plate.

*   *   *

Tonight I'll jerk off thinking about Abe's girl Mandy. She came by a few days ago when Abe was with mom at the doctor's.

"Where's Abe?" she asked when I opened the door, her hands on her waist, her chin sunk toward her breasts.

"Gone," I said.

She threw a glance over my shoulder. My hand was still on the door.

"Gonna let me in?" she asked. She brushed past me in the entry and my hand dropped from the door. I followed. She climbed the stairs and I stared as we rose. We walked into my brother's room. She placed a small box on his desk.

"Ever think it's weird?" She pointed to the shelves that housed my brother's Zippos.

"I don't give it much thought," I said.

Mandy put her hands in her blue jean pockets and lowered her eyes. "What *do* you think about?"

I couldn't think an answer.

"Why ain't you got a girlfriend, Jardon?" She smiled and my face got hot. I looked at Charlie. I counted the points on his antlers. One, two, three, four.

"Um," I said. Five, six.

"Abe says it's cause you're scared." She ran her fingers down the buttons of her shirt.

Seven, eight. "Um." Nine, ten.

Mandy laughed and clapped her hands together. She shook them as though finishing a prayer and let them fall to her sides. "I reckon he's right," she said and walked from the room. I heard her feet on the steps. Eleven. I heard her at the door. Twelve.

My brother runs hurdles. The other runners call him Hot Mess. He's first in district. I think the other runners get distracted by the scar tissue that wraps his head. Mom says he's driven. She goes to all his meets. That and the doctor's only trips she makes. She sits near the track. She hacks and hollers while Abe's legs pump, his back pitched, neck cocked, lips slack, body flailing, then pinching as his knees pull up and he floats over the hurdles.

Once my mother asked him how. "How you run so fast?" I was lying on the sofa. It was winter. We'd built a fire. The logs cracked, shrinking as they peeled away as smoke. My eyes were warm. They seemed to peel away too. My brother started to answer. "Well," he said. "I always imagine," his voice turned soft as my eyes sunk, but my ears were open, and they must've spun his words into dream, because I dreamt my brother was on the starting line wearing animal-hide shorts, barefoot, with gold chains round his wrists and a giant fire yards behind him. Then a tank, a Panzer like the ones in *Patton*, drew near the line and the cabin opened and a man with spikes for eyes rose from the tank, and said, "The loser burns." Then there were other racers. Black men with naked bodies and speed skaters with skin-tight get ups and a cheetah with giant teeth. Then the drums rolling like anxiety, and the man in the tank began to laugh. "On your mark," my brother lowered his burnt skull and touched his toes, "Set," my brother's buttocks raised slightly and the cheetah growled, "Go," the tank fired a blank and the racers exploded from the line. The skaters hissed across their ice. The cheetah bounded the track. The black men's penises jangled as their knees rose and fell. But then my brother, running, his face coming toward me. Then just my brother with his back to a fire and sprinting. Then just his face, strands of flesh like red yarn unraveling as the fire chased a loose thread back toward the bundle of his head and the bundle laughed as it floated away as ash and ribbons of smoke, and all of this was done with speed.

*   *   *

Jim and I walk home after school. I guess you could say Jim's my best friend, but that would imply that I have several friends, and I don't. There's just Jim.

I hear my brother's American Scout, fitted with glass pack exhaust, clapping like a jack hammer down the road. He pulls up beside us and revs his engine. The glass packs clap and his girl Hillary, sitting in the passenger's seat, laughs and throws her arm around my brother's neck.

"What you fags doing?" my brother asks. Then Hillary laughs again and kisses his cheek.

"Walking," Jim says. He points in the direction we're headed. "Unless you wanna give us a ride?"

"Let me think," my brother says. He hits the gas and screams shrill. "Later fags." The Scout claps away and Hillary's laughter peals from her window.

"It's homosexual," Jim yells out after the Scout shrinking from view. He shakes his head, rolls his eyes and looks at me. I slide my feet on the pavement away from Jim.

My mother's emphysema keeps her perched on the sofa in the living room with her black pen in hand and a crossword sprawled across her weakening legs.

Sometimes she'll get stumped and cough out, "Four," hiss hiss, "letter," hiss, "word for calefaction."

She always needs words for other words.

Sometimes I'll go in and sit with her and look the puzzles over, but most of the times I go in I get the urge to ask about Dad.

"Have you heard from him?" I'll ask.

"Called," hiss hiss, "the other," hiss, "day."

"What'd he say?"

"Just," hiss, "some stuff." Eyes roll. Hiss. Cough. Snap of phlegm. Towel toward lips and spitting. "Kind of interesting."

I nod and leave. Interesting's her word for another word.

My brother's in the garage bouncing a racquetball against the oil-stained floor. His girl Tiffany sits on an overturned milk crate doodling on lined paper that lies across her knees. I pull the door soft behind me, but the latch snaps and my brother looks up. He sends the ball toward the floor with heat, so it floats up, taps the ceiling, then lands in his opened palm.

"Help you?" my brother asks.

Tiffany's eyes on the page.

"I got a question," I tell him.

My brother looks back down at the floor and bounces the ball coolly. "Shoot," he says.

"I was wanting maybe to ask you alone," I say.

My brother looks over at Tiffany. Her eyes still on the page. "I might as well be alone now," he says and thumps the ball against the ground. Tiffany doodles.

I rub my hands on my elbows and lean my head toward my brother. "It's Jim," I say.

"Oh yeah," my brother says and touches his free hand to the scars of his skull. "What about him?"

I'm standing on a Florida shaped oil stain. "I think he's queer," I say.

"Come again," my brother says and catches the ball.

"Queer," I tell him. "But I'm not sure."

Bounce. "Ask him." Bounce. Bounce.

"Seems a wrong thing to ask."

Bounce. "You're friends ain't you?" Bounce. Bounce.

Tiffany looks up from her doodling and says, "There's some things you ain't supposed to do."

My brother catches the ball and looks at

Tiffany. He puts the ball in his pocket and reaches for his wrist. He's wearing a bracelet that he unclasps. He dangles it in the air at me, but he's still looking at Tiffany.

"Give him this," he says.

"A bracelet?"

"Sure," says my brother. "Only a fag would wear a bracelet a boy gave em."

I take the bracelet from my brother's hand. "Where'd you get it?" I ask.

"My girl Mandy gave it to me," he says, his eyes on Tiffany who looks up when he says the name. "That's right," he says. "You're one of dozens."

Sometimes at dusk I'll walk the road down to Corpus Christi Bay to watch the sun dip out away from the Harbor Bridge and watch the clouds and smog climbing from the oil refineries run from pink to purple to gray once the sun finally sets. My father used to bring me down here and point over to the buildings downtown while I skipped oyster shells across the salt water. He'd tell me names of people who worked in them, and names of people in the news, and how the folks in the buildings knew the news folks, and how that was the only way to get the jobs in the buildings and that that was why he'd been out of work so long.

"I just don't know nobody," he'd say.

When he was like that I couldn't look at him. I'd look out across the salt water to the blur of coast across the water or count the sailboats with their white sails stuffed with evening's wind, and all the while the gulls would crack their caws.

Lacey Pratter's feet, worn and busted. Her toes like salted almonds dangling from the desktop. She leans back on her elbows and puts her hands on her hips.

"I wouldn't figure you one," she says.

We're in the portables behind the school learning study skills from a half-drunk teacher. I'm thumping an eraser against the same table on which Pratter sits.

"One what?" I ask.

There are ten of us in the class, including the teacher, and Pratter and I are the only ones with heads up.

"My uncle was one," she says. "Sammy. But you could tell with him a mile off. Something in his strut."

"Strut?" I ask. "Like a chicken?"

"Prettier feathers," says Pratter. "Colors and all."

Pratter's knees are bruised and her fingernails are bit to quick.

"Some chickens got colors," I tell her. "Rhode Island Reds are nice to look at."

Pratter drags her teeth at a nail but it doesn't catch. "I guess you notice good, and that's part of it," she says. "Sammy was always noticing new stuff that mom put out and my shoes."

We both look at Pratter's feet.

"You know," she says, "if I was wearing shoes."

"Notice stuff?"

"Yeah, like the color of chickens."

"Everyone knows Reds," I tell her. "They lay the brown eggs that come in the fiber cartons. Not like the whites in Styrofoam."

"There again," she says. "Details."

"I guess," I tell her.

"Like Gully," she says, and points to a boy two desks away. His puny face rests on folded arms, his pale eyelids shut. "He's got more the look."

I look at his skimp cheeks. "Gully was on my tee ball team," I say. "He played first base."

Pratter looks at me and winks. "I get it," she says. "Code."

"Code for what?"

"For whatever you folks consider first base," she says.

"Pratter, you never watched baseball?"

"I seen Sammy tongue kiss his boyfriend Hank once after Thanksgiving."

"Pratter'd, you leave your brain with your shoes?"

Pratter slips from the desk top. "Sorry," she says, "Didn't realize the topic was so touchy."

"What topic?"

"I just figured you gave Jim that bracelet and so y'all was open bout it."

I've been trying to teach myself electric piano cause I want to start a band, but so far I can only play a few bits of hymns and improvise some so long as I keep it in the key of C. The hymns I learned from a hymnal I swiped from Jim's church, and I looked up the names of the notes and where to find them on the keyboard from a book in my school's library.

I just got the piano last Christmas. I haven't played it for anybody yet. It's got an earphone jack that I stay plugged into while I'm practicing. There's a framed poster that hangs on the wall in front of where I play, and the mounting of the poster is black, so I can see my face in the reflection of the glass. I practice my looks in the reflection while I noodle the keys. I try to hold my face like Spencer Krug. I know the words to all Wolf Parade's songs, but I can only play "When the Saints Go Marching In."

Abe's barebacked in the yard with a scimitar in his left hand and a tooth pick in his lips. There's a deer hanging from its hind quarter, tied to a hook in the tree. Abe runs the blade down the belly of the buck so its guts leap forward from the cavity and land like noodles in a metal bowl in the grass. The bowl chimes. Abe reaches for a sharpening steel that sits on a stool beside him. He holds it in his free hand pointed toward his shoes and runs the blade down the shaft in swift strokes. The blade chirps against the steel. The deer sways in a low breeze to the left until the rope stiffens, then to the right, and back, its antlers like antennae at the ground.

"You fucked me up, Abe," I say and push his shoulder.

Abe looks at the blade. He rolls the tooth pick across his lips with his tongue. He hits the blade against the steel. He moves toward the deer.

The gate to the yard opens. We both look. A girl named Valerie steps into the yard. She slams the gate and smiles and waves and heads through the grass toward Abe. She stops a few inches from him and squares her hips to his. She looks into his face and licks her lips then kneels and Abe shucks back his shoulders, raising knife and steel toward the sky, rolling his burnt head on his neck. Valerie crouches for a moment, then rises with the bowl, guts brimming, and turns to head back for the gate. She flings the bowl into one hand, flips the latch on the gate, and disappears through it.

Abe hits the blade against the steel once more before setting the steel back on the stool. He takes hold of the deer's hide with his free hand and, with the knife working in long smooth strokes, draws the hide off the body, chasing the blade below the hide toward the deer's backbone.

"How'd I fuck you up?" He doesn't look at me. His attention's on the deer.

"The bracelet," I say, "Jim wore the stupid thing, and told folks where he got it and now everyone figures I'm that way."

"Well," says Abe, and rolls the pick in his mouth, "only a fag'd give a boy a bracelet."

"The fuck," I tell him. "Only done what you said."

"Shit," says Abe, he lets the knife free from his hand and it stays in the deer. "What you want to do about it?" Abe wipes both hands against his chest, streaking himself with blood, and he cracks his neck by rocking his burnt head. The deer swings mildly in the low breeze, and the handle of the scimitar rolls with it, pointing out like a finger.

The handle points at me, "I want it fixed."

The handle points at Abe, "How you suppose that's gonna happen?"

The handle points at me, "You're gonna tell folks you gave the bracelet to Jim."

The handle points at Abe, "You've lost your wits."

Abe pulls the knife from the deer hide and looks at the bloody blade. "Why not get yourself a girl?" Abe asks. "Clear the debate." Beads of blood fall from the blade to the grass.

"Ain't that easy," I say.

"Sure it is," he tells me. "I've seen you talking to that Pratter."

"Shit," I say, "I ain't dating Pratter."

"Course you ain't," he tells me. "You need to get yourself something with shoes." My brother takes the knife back to the buck. "But if she'll talk to you, any girl will talk to you. That's how they is."

"Huh?"

"If one girl likes you half a dozen do at least. They function like a network."

I didn't know if he was right but I liked the way it sounded, so I sat Indian style in the grass and watched my brother skin the buck.

Mr. Fotter. Pot bellied and red faced. His nose blossomed from drink and his head shiny bald. We're in the portables. The air is humid. The lights are fluorescent. There is a constant hum from a window unit purring. Fotter stands off balance in front of the class, rocking gently in his fake leather shoes, absently rubbing his belly, trying to teach.

"It's not that you become what you are. But there are skills you need. Things to be done, if you want to become something. It takes desire. It takes work. You need ethic, too. If you want to be anything. And organized. It's necessary to be organized. There has to be, and not just on occasion, a demonstration shown. Organization. Planning. Promptness."

Gully's eyelids heave.

"When I was in the military," Fotter pauses, hands on gut. "Have I told you about the military?"

Pratter nods her head and thumbs a toe.

"Yes, of course. In the morning early, every day. Up with the sun. And out running," Fotter looks at his belly. "Maybe could stand some now. But in my prime, every day. And you youngsters. You're in your prime. So every day."

"You want us to run?"

The class snickers.

"In some respects, young man, yes. Run through the motions. Prompt. Organized. On time. Groomed."

Gully's eyes are closed.

"It takes work to get to where you want to be. I had to work to be this. I wanted to be a fighter pilot, but I had bad eyes, but I didn't give up. I was on the USS Lexington. The same that's now lodged in the bay. Years ago. Boy it was a fine ship. Out. On the ocean with the fellas. Twenty foot seas. Salt spray and sea air. Charging the water. Me and the fellas. Rocking the boat did. All bunked up together. And whew we charged those seas, God bless the U.S.A."

Gully's head rests on his desk.

*　　　*　　　*

If they are a network then they need reprogramming, because I tried a mess of them and they all slid away like I slid from Jim when I first got the suspicion, though I don't know what they supposed I was other than something to get away from. Which they did.

Tina, Jessica, Dorene, Molly, Wynona, Winter, Stephanie, Heather, Holly, Brooke, Justine, Eliza, Jennifer and a Dutch exchange student named Adelheid. Slid like the floor was Vaselined and I'd pushed them.

Wait. One girl. Adelheid. She first came in close. Made me repeat myself.

"Again," she said. Batted her eyes and I thought I was in.

"Want to go around," I said.

"What?"

"Go around."

"Well," she said. "Go around what?"

"Oh," I said. "Go around with me."

"I don't get," she said. Then a friend whispered in her ear and they both laughed and walked down the hall.

Gasoline feels a bit like soft water, and the fumes make your head echo and rattle as though your skull was a burnt out light bulb being shook. I don't know why I'd never thought of it before. I was at the piano practicing hymnals and practicing faces in the glass of the poster on the wall. Mom and Abe had gone for a doctor's visit, and so I'd pulled the earphones from the jack and had the volume turned up so high that the poster was shaking on the nail it hung from when I pressed the low notes, and my face looked mottled in the shake, and I suppose I liked the look better cause all of a sudden I got to thinking about the gasoline in the garage, and then I wasn't playing, I was taking off my shirt and folding it and placing it on my bed. Then I looked in the poster. Me. I pressed the keys. Me with mottled face. "Fuck it," I thought. "Couldn't get worse." So I rose from the piano and went into my brother's room. I walked to the shelf where he kept his lighters. Lighters of all kinds. Lighters with motorcycle logos, and beer logos, and pictures with sayings like, "Life's a Beach," or, "Great Balls of Fire." I grabbed a silver one because I could kind of see my face in it and I walked down the stairs looking into it, and I couldn't wait until the flesh looking back was different. I went down the stairs and out to the garage and grabbed the gasoline can and poured a good douse on my head, and it ran like sweat from my hair and down my face, and it felt like death in the eyes. I took a few breaths. The vapors change you quick, change your balance, change your pitch. Then it's my face in the lighter staring back at me wet. Wet hair. Wet cheeks. Then my face, gone, flipped back in the cap, and the hinge clicking, and the wick in the windscreen, and I put my thumb on the wheel. I breathe deep the gas. The saints are still marching in my ears from the playing. I try to hold my face like something. I try to hold it cool. Then. Nothing.

I thumb the wheel and it spins. Nothing. I thumb it again. Nothing. Nothing. I thumb the wheel. Nothing. I close it, and open it, and thumb it, and nothing. I shake it, thumb it. Nothing. I shake it again and let it fall from my hand. Then, dizzy, moving with the new gasoline pitch up the steps into Abe's room, winking at Charley, who may be winking at me, and at the shelf with the lighters, and the lighters, the one that says Navy and the ones with slogans, and logos, and mottos and names of strangers, dates, cities, skulls, snakes, and flipping the caps, and thumbing them all, and nothing, and nothing, and dropped from my hand, and nothing, and nothing, and thumbing and nothing. And thumbing. And nothing. And dropped. All dropped, dozens near my feet on the carpet. My head wet and wreaking of vapors and flesh not mottled.

My hair's still damp when Jim comes to the door. He stands on the porch still wearing the bracelet.

"Your hair's wet," he says. The sun's beginning to set, and Jim's pale hair looks pink in the color of it.

I look down the street. "Wanna go to the bay?" I ask.

"Sure," he says, and we step off the porch and head for the saltwater.

I look at him again. He doesn't strike me in any way. But I do contemplate him.

Pretty
good
↳ identity

MY SECOND THROAT

I didn't come back from the war because I knew you'd be waiting for me. I found the enemy and spat in his eye. It surprised him. My spit slinking down his cheek. He had a pistol. He cocked it and placed the barrel against my throat. He sort of chewed his bottom lip before squeezing the trigger. I could taste the bullet move through me. I thought I'd choke on my blood. I slumped to the ground gasping and I'm near certain he kicked twice at my chest before whistling and walking away. I writhed there. I tried timing my pulse. A shadow took everything. I dreamt I'd swallowed myself through a second throat and I dreamt there were hands the size of grown men messing my hair. I woke on a gurney. An up and down motion. Then I was back down my second throat and beneath an umbrella spinning. I woke in a room so bright my white bed sheet burnt my eyes. All around me the stench of dampened gauze. A doctor preached my luck to me. He told me in less capable hands I would have been doomed. He smiled and a full-chested nurse touched his shoulder. I wanted to thank him. But my throat was a bruised cage door. I was in the hospital for months. I played checkers with an amputee. I had to move his pieces for him. I had to ash his cigarette in a coffee can. I wanted to smoke with him. I still cannot talk right. On my last day in hospital they sang me a song. I tried singing along with them but my voice is a minced mouse tail. I came to your house once. I stood at your doorstep. I slicked my hair back with thick gel and hid my scar beneath an ascot and wore fancy cologne. I don't know what I was hoping for. I didn't even want to talk to you. Maybe I wanted to see what you'd done with yourself or maybe I wanted to see if you'd moved from the house or maybe I wanted to see the color of the man that you took or maybe I wanted to see if you'd carried to term. I got your letter. I'm glad you didn't come find me. At the park children come to sit at my feet and if they give me a nickel I'll let them see where they got me. I'll pull aside my ascot and they can touch where the bullet hit. I don't think the kids like me. One of them pissed on my shoes once. I pretended it was our kid. The one that we'd made together and then that made it better because that made it worth it. Who would want to live with that? Who would want to be part of that? Who would want to share that with you? Not me. And anyhow my shoes are dry now and I think things are getting better. I've got a pocket heavy with nickels and I've got place that I'm going to. There's a song on a radio. I can pretend to sing along with it.

Awesome

PALE MILK

I

Come afternoon Jeffrey's mother will hold the screen door open, and her boy will step through. Out, onto the stoop, his eyes tired in their sockets, a stilted smile pulled across his face like a piece of wet string. He'll take the steps in twos, letting his feet fall against the cement. His body will pitch like a car antennae in the wind. He'll put his toes in the grass, hands held out like airplane wings. His mother will let the door slam. The neighbors will give their attention. Watching as the young man moves awkward toward a length of cable stretched head-high between a pair of oaks. A leash. Custom fitted with a spring latch on each end, at the center of the cable, ten feet from either tree. Jeffrey will zigzag toward it. He will clip the free latch to his belt loop. He'll step toward his father's house and the leash will draw down the line.

II

Two men touch bottlenecks on the porch.
"This is living."
"This is."
"Jeffrey's gone all summer?"
"All summer. Camp in the hills. Special training? Something."
"I thought his kind was smart."

"He's good at the puzzles."
There is a dull silence as both men drink.
"Well, least there's that."

III

Wet leaves rot in mounds on either side of Jeffrey's path. Jeffrey in a navy slicker that glistens with sleet. The air big. Chimney smoke. Dead leaves. Hot hard cider which births steam from cups. Across the street a neighbor girl sits on a Trans Am hood smoking menthol cigarettes. Her boyfriend stands between her spread legs with his back toward her. The girl strokes his long hair. Jeffrey walks from tree to tree. Watching.

"What's wrong with him?"

"Don't know. Short bus picks him up. Wakes me up every fucking morning." She flicks at the butt of her cigarette. Ashes drift in the wind.

"How old is he?"

"Younger than me, but I used to play with him."

The boyfriend turns and takes the girl's cigarette.

"Yeah," he says and takes a drag. "What'd you play?"

"Doctor," she says, and waves at Jeffrey. "We played doctor."

The boyfriend laughs. Smoke pours from his smile. Jeffrey hides his face in his hand and walks from tree to tree.

IV

She. She. She. She. She. She. She. She. She. She. She. She. She. She. She. She. She. She. She. She. She. She. She. She. She. She. She. She. She. She. She. She. She. She. She. She. She. She. She. She.

V

"At first I figured she was drunk. Kept on pounding at the door with her fist. Must have woken up half the street. And if she didn't the dogs did, cause they heard her racket and got to barking. Personally I don't give a shit how bad a father he is. He's a man with a job, got work next morning and she lives off the state. Anyhow, he flipped on the light and came out in his night clothes, and she started hollering about *his* son being sick. So he stepped down off the porch and the both of them went into her house. If you ask me it's a shit situation for a man to find himself in."

VI

Two men touch bottlenecks on the porch. The street is quiet save the muffled groaning of a female.

"Trans Am boy must give it to her hard."

"Shit. All that long hair. Didn't figure he had it in him."

Dull silence. Drinking.

"Hell. I wish I was young again."

"Not me. Nothing but trouble." He points to Jeffrey who drifts from tree to tree.

A door opens across the street. The groaning girl steps weary into the sunshine and lights a menthol cigarette.

One of the beer drinkers waves at her. She shows him her middle finger.

VII

"On Wednesday evenings he'll come down off his porch. He'll walk the path to the sidewalk, turn right, then turn up her path and go up to her door.

He'll knock. She'll let him in. I suppose they have dinner cause he's always dressed up a bit, and he stays in there for a stretch of time. First time I saw it I figured he was going to propose. It was the way he was dressed and all. The way his face was quiet. How he held his hands. He didn't. Or if he did she said no. I keep expecting one of them to put their house for sale and move away."

VIII

A new neighbor. Walking with tight pants on. Coming quick. Stepping in rhythm. Pulling hands high as she moves. Face red. Deep breathing. Listening to music and humming along. She stops when she sees Jeffrey. She plants a foot and her body lunges forward. The motion messes her balance. She stumbles and almost trips, but catches herself with awkward footwork, steadies herself, then crosses her arms.

"Boy, why you leashed?" Her voice is louder than it needs to be. She takes her headphones off and waits for an answer. Jeffrey is quiet.

"What's that ma'am?" A man on the porch of the neighboring house sets a beer beside him on the pavement.

"The boy," says the woman. "He's leashed."

"Yes ma'am," the man says. "Every afternoon," he says and points to Jeffrey. "He ain't normal."

"So, you leash him?" the woman says. She moves closer to the boy, who walks undisturbed from tree to tree.

"Oh," says the man. "No ma'am," he laughs. "The boy leashes himself."

The woman is on the lawn. She's moving closer to Jeffrey. Jeffrey stops. He stares at her.

"I used to have a lab," the man says. "The line was for it. But he got off one day and disappeared, and the boy started clipping himself to it, so I never cut it down."

"It's inhumane," the woman says. "He shouldn't be leashed like an animal."

The woman moves slow toward Jeffrey. She drops her shoulders and extends her hands. "Shush," she says. "It's okay," she tells him. "This isn't right."

The woman reaches for the spring clip which is hooked to one of Jeffrey's belt loops. She snaps the clip and thrusts the leash down the line. It bobs and bounces in the air. The woman steps back. Jeffrey looks at her. He bites his lip. He touches his palms. He walks down to the leash and clips it back on his pants.

IX

She came out of her house first. He followed close by. They carried their argument into the street. He put his hand on her shoulder, but she brushed it off, then he tried for her waist but she wriggled free.

"I don't get you."

"Nothing to get."

She got some distance, then turned to face him. "You're pestering me."

"Is that what you'd call it?"

"I would," she said. He reached for her hand, but she pulled back. "It's like strangulation."

"There someone else?"

"Sure," she said. She looked over her shoulder. "Jeffrey." She pointed at the boy pacing between the trees.

"Shit," he said. He laughed. "Prove it."

She smiled at him. She began to unbutton her blouse.

"What the hell you doing?" he asked. He moved forward. She moved back.

She undid the buttons quickly and spread her flannel shirt open, so that her breasts were bared. She turned and walked toward Jeffrey who stood still and watched.

When she reached him she put her arm around his waist. Jeffrey put his hands to his face. The boy got in his Trans Am and sped down the road.

X

She. She. She. She. She. She. She. She. She. She. She. She. She. She. She. She. She. She. She. She. She. She. She. She. She. She. She. She. She. She. She. She. She. She. She. She. She. She. She. She.

XI

The tickets were fifty dollars a piece. Jeffrey's mother talked him into it.

"It'll do him good to get out in public."

"He gets plenty of public at the school."

Eventually persuaded, he figured he'd do it right. Got good seats behind the home-team dugout. Got Jeffrey a Nolan Ryan jersey, a giant soda and some popcorn. Showed the boy a score sheet and how to make the marks. But he didn't get it. Didn't care much for the game. Made it through the first two batters then turned around in his chair. Sat watching the woman behind him the whole time they were there. Eyes latched on her breasts. Made his father nervous.

"Don't mind the boy," he told the woman. "His mother had pale milk."

Nobody laughed.

XII

"Used to they'd pay the girl to watch him, or at least that's what the girl's mother told me. Said they'd give her three bucks an hour, and she'd go over there and they'd play, or whatever. I don't know exactly why it stopped. I don't think there was anything unusual. Maybe she got older and developed interests. I don't know. I do know she's a bit loose, and I seen her do some questionable things. Maybe the boy's mother was afraid she'd be a bad influence. Maybe money got tight and she realized it didn't do no good no how. I'm not friends with his mother. I say hi from time to time, but she keeps to herself and I do the same."

XIII

The two men have gone through an awful lot of beer. There are empty bottles on the porch and in the grass. One of them has a harmonica. From time to time he mouths a few notes. Their speech is messy, and they are loud. Their voices can be heard down the street. One of the men has just come back from a baseball game. The Astros lost. He keeps repeating the score.

"It was a mess, and I dumped a pile of money."

"Sounds it."

The man with the harmonica breathes a quick riff.

"You know, I didn't cum in his momma."

"What?"

"Not proper. It was the first time she had me over. She'd only lived next door a few weeks. We were drinking wine, and things lead to things. But I think I drank too much, cause I thrashed around, and we tried for a long while, but nothing of it."

Dull. Drunk.

"Then you ain't the daddy?"

"No, I is."

"How you figure?"

"He's all dribble and no dynamite. The doctor explained it to me, said it happens sometimes."

"Huh. You think that's why?"

"Might be. Doctor says he doubts it. But I don't think they know much. I wish she would have pulled the plug on the thing like I asked."

"At least moved."

A Trans Am rolls slow down the road. One of the men tips a bottle back and chugs his beer. He pulls the bottle from his lips. Beer sprays into the air, and he breathes heavy as though he's emerged from a swimming pool for air. A few notes are played on the harmonica.

"This boy here don't know what he's getting into."

"Oh, I get the feeling he knows." The men chuckle.

"No. In the long run."

"Well, he'll make some mistakes. It'll come clear to him."

The Trans Am parks on the street. One of the men rises from the porch. He steps down into the yard and lets an empty bottle fall from his hand. It hits the grass. There is a dull tone as it rolls to a rest.

The door to the Trans Am opens. The driver gets out. His feet scrape the asphalt. He closes the door behind him and circles the car and heads toward the girl's house.

"Hey, Trans Am," the man says. "Where you going?"

Trans Am boy turns. He looks surprised. He points at the house behind him.

"No you ain't," the man says. "Nothing but trouble in there."

The harmonica fills the street with slow notes.

The boy shakes his head. He squints his eyes. He whispers, "You drunk?"

"Might be," says the man.

Trans Am boy laughs. He heads up the cement walk to the door of the house.

It's too late when he hears the footsteps. The man's shoulder hits the small of his back, and the two go down into the grass.

The slow notes cease. There are grunts and groans coming from the grass. Dogs begin to bark. House lights come on.

They continue tussling. The boy breaks free. He stands and heads for the house. The man grabs his ankle. He pulls him back to the grass.

More grunts. More groans. More dogs barking. More lights.

Again the boy breaks free. He stands. The man is between him and the house. They are both breathing heavy. The boy shakes his hands. He spits on the ground and walks to his car.

"You're crazy," he says. He gets in the Trans Am and drives away slow.

XIV

"The girl was outside smoking cigarettes. She was sitting on the curb like an Indian, and she kept looking both ways like she was expecting something, but nothing came. It was afternoon. Jeffrey's mother let him out the screen door and he come down and latched himself. Everything was normal. Him going back from tree to tree. Then he looked over at the girl who was smoking and stood still. It took a bit, but she noticed him. She smiled. Seemed embarrassed. She set her cigarette down, stood up and waved at him. Then Jeffrey waved back. He waved. At the girl, he did. He waved on back."

ACCIDENT FINGER

When I pray, I pray for untraceable cash. Judith keeps the credit cards in her billfold. She's based the account passwords on birthdates I'm unaware of. She put the house in her name, and her father mows the lawn now. She runs wide spread fingers through her pale blonde hair when she sees me. She breathes deep and shakes her hot head quick and small and swirls her eyes and clicks her teeth. There are restrictions now I'm back from treatment. I have to check in. I've got a phone that only dials her number. I've got a chart on the refrigerator that I'm supposed to mark with an X when we talk.

"Do you know what your word's worth?" she says when I promise to be good if she lets me go to the playground to shoot basketball. "Nothing," she answers for me.

I nod. I open my mouth. I trace the lines on the floor with my nubbed finger and rest my head on the receiver as I lay on the ground.

"Is there something you want to say to me?" she'll ask.

"Sure," I say and I stare at the floor. "What do you think grout's made of?"

Then she hangs up the telephone.

I got a fever in the treatment. My hands felt like sea shells, but I couldn't hear the ocean in them. I couldn't swallow and I stood in the hallway outside my room and the night nurses circled me and asked me where I was headed.

"I need medicine," I told them. "My throat's broken."

One of the women nurses used a cell phone to call the doctors. I didn't understand what she said. I tried listening for the ocean again. It wasn't working. I held my hand to one of the male nurse's ears, but he flinched away, and their circle swallowed me. They mashed my hands against my back and drove my chest to the ground. They gave each other high fives while on their knees beside me, and they panted, and flustered, and after a few minutes they asked me if I was ready to stand. I nodded, but I was confused because I had already been standing when they grabbed me. Then they pulled me up by my elbows and walked me to the end of the hall. There was a camera mounted on the ceiling with a red light on its face that blinked. It turned from side to side as though shaking its head. I could sort of see us, reflected in its giant black eye. I smiled as we passed beneath it and one of the nurses asked me what was so funny.

On Friday Judith will fly to Florida to attend a conference. Her plane leaves early. I never leave the house now. Her father is staying the weekend with me. Judith says he has to work on the lawn. Judith takes me to the kitchen and holds my arm and opens the pantry. She shows me where the bread and sodas are. She pulls me to the refrigerator. She points to the lunch meat. She points to the mayonnaise.

"Got it?" she asks.

I nod. I open my mouth.

"What?" she says.

I whisper, "How do you think they make mayonnaise?"

Then Judith slams the refrigerator door and leaves the room.

The air in the room the nurses took me to felt smooth and cool. It was dim. Only the echo of a pale light haunted the white walls and mattress. The nurses laid me down and withdrew. They didn't see it, but a pencil dropped from behind one of their ears as they lowered me. I waited until they were gone before I picked it up.

Here's the last prayer I prayed:

Dear God, please give me untraceable cash. Last time you left the credit card on the kitchen counter, which was kind of you, but I got caught, and Judith still hasn't forgiven me, and now I have a stupid phone that just knows one number, and I have to X the chart, and Judith talks more with the doctors, and she still hasn't told me what she thinks grout is made from, and I ask her almost every day. Also, I know what mayonnaise is made from. It's made from eggs and oil. But Judith doesn't know that. I bet she thinks it's made from milk. Amen.

If I start as soon as Judith leaves in the morning I can trace all the grout in the house in a single day. I like to use my accident finger, the one I clipped with the mower, but maybe that's because it was my favorite finger to begin with. Judith doesn't like me to do it. She threatens to get carpet. Right now we've got green tile. The lines are like a graph of rivers that have dried on the surface of a planet made from chalkboards. I know that tiny people don't live in the grout lines, but sometimes I pretend. Sometimes I even spill a cup of water, and watch the water crawl through the grout lines, and

I imagine the tiny people running from the wall of
water that's racing across their itsy-bitsy homes. I
don't know what grout's made of, but I pretend it's
made from a moon. Not our moon though, that's
silly, our moon's still there, but someone else's
moon, that maybe we flew across the universe for.

It was almost perfect when they took away
the pencil. There were things that needed to be
extended and erased, but for the most part it was
perfect. The shading was the best I'd ever done.
All of the eyes looked like hers and mine. There
was a tree, and I'd done each leaf like a real leaf,
and I even put how the roots sunk into the ground
just the same as in real life. Every blade of grass,
because I had so much time, every blade of grass
I did individual. Some people lay the pencil tip on
its side and just go back and forth, so the grass
looks like a million rivers or snakes, but I had so
much time that I did every blade the way I could
remember them, and I even did three types of
clouds and two types of birds, and all of the shingles
and the bricks in the chimney, I just hadn't gotten
to the clothes yet, and that's when they took away
the sheets and showed them to Judith, and I think
it's why she hates me now, and I think it's why my
phone can only call her phone.

"What about the money?" I say.
Judith turns. "Excuse me?"
"You know," I say. "In case of emergency?"
The muscles in Judith's face tighten and her
skin makes itself red. "Emergency?" she says, and
runs her fingers through her hair.
"Sure," I say. "Like fire, or something."
Judith fake laughs. It sounds like her throat is
pretending to hold a bird. "Why not," she says and

she reaches for her purse. She pulls out her billfold.
She holds it against her chest the way fat women
hold candy bars. She unclasps the wallet latch and
lowers her pinchers. She pulls out a single dollar
bill and lays it on the table. "There you go," she
says. "All the money you'll need." Then she goes
outside and gets in her car to drive to the airport.

Judith's father watches car racing with the
volume off. "So," he says. "Do you even know what's
going on?"

I look at the television. It's like dozens of cars
are pretending to be a carnival ride. "Circles," I tell
him, and he sips at his beer.

"Circles," he says.

"Yup," I say. "Round and round."

Judith's father shakes his head. He looks at
my shoes. "Is that Velcro?" he asks.

I reach down. I pull on a band and the Velcro
cracks like static. "Velcro's exactly what it is," I
say.

Judith's father changes the channel a
thousand times before coming back to the car
racing. I put my hand in my pocket and rub
my dollar. I pretend I'm messing with George
Washington's hair. I pretend he leans into it, like
when you scratch behind the ear of a dog. "Good,
George Washington," I think to myself, accept I
mess up and accidentally say it out loud.

"What?" Judith's father says. He leans
towards me. His eyes narrow and his lips shrink
like a tightening fist.

I look to my right. I look to my left. I put my
hand on my chest. "Who me?" I ask.

Judith and I got married after high school. I
didn't have to go to college because my dad left me

two million dollars. I didn't cry much when he died because he was really old. People used to ask if he was my grandfather, and, if I didn't feel like explaining, I'd just nod my head yes. Judith sat behind me in algebra, and I didn't understand algebra, and she'd help me with the graphs. After the wedding we went on a honeymoon to a resort in Costa Rica with a bar that you could swim up to, and you could order drinks served in real life coconuts and there were monkeys that played on a tree that had penis shaped limbs. We called it the penis tree and Judith screamed at the monkeys, "Hoo, hoo, hoo." We played a game in the pool to see who could hold their breath the longest, and we went to the top of a volcano, and did a canopy tour where we flew through the rainforest on wires that we clipped to our belts, and we went down to the ocean and found seashells, and we went to a sanctuary where a man with a mustache let us hold parrots that made all kinds of sounds. Back then Judith didn't run her fingers through her hair, and my phone could call anybody you could think of. Then one night, and I mean years after the honeymoon, we were at a carnival and we were eating cotton candy, and then I was watching the Ferris wheel and it started going backwards, and Judith didn't understand what I was saying, but what I was saying was so simple, because the Ferris wheel was going backwards, but she only shook her head, so we had to go closer so I could explain, but the closer we got the less she understood, and I even kept telling her and pointing, and motioning backwards, and backwards I'd tell her, but it was loud with the games and the music and the children running between us, but I kept saying it, I couldn't have been any plainer. "Backwards," I told her. "Backwards," I said.

Judith's father is wearing shorts and loafers. He has on protective goggles. He holds a beer in one hand, and the fingers of his other hand are tucked in his elastic waistband. I sit on the sofa with my feet on the coffee table. The television is off, but I like to watch my reflection in it. It looks like a ghost of me. When I wave it waves back.

"I'm going outside," Judith's father says. "I'm going outside to do your job."

I scratch my head. "I don't mow the lawn anymore," I tell him and show him the missing tip of my finger.

"No shit," he says. He drains his beer and sets it down on the coffee table. Then he brushes my feet to the ground. I sit up on the sofa. So does the TV me. Judith's father goes to the kitchen and opens the refrigerator door. I hear him take a beer from the refrigerator and twist the cap. It sounds like the bottle wants to tell him a secret. He opens the trash can and drops in the bottle top. It sounds like a coin tossed into a dried up fountain. He comes back into the living room. "I'll be outside for an hour or so," he says. "You think you can stay out of trouble."

"I stay at home by myself a lot," I tell him. He shakes his head. I put my feet back on the coffee table.

Judith's father goes out the garage door and I hear the big door being drawn up by the motor. I wait for a bit. When I hear the lawnmower engine coughing across the front yard I slip out the back door and hop the back fence. I don't even think about it. As soon as my feet hit the alley's asphalt I'm sprinting.

My father apologized on his death bed for not leaving me the money in cash. "What you'd really want is cash, because it's untraceable, but there's no real way to do that anymore. In the movies, sure," he said. "In the movies there's always a guy walking around with a briefcase of hundreds, but I asked my lawyers and they advised against it because it would look suspicious, you getting a briefcase of cash from your father just before he died and all, so I've got the money all set up in accounts, so they'll all know where it is. If it was cash you could do whatever you wanted to with it. You could buy anything you wanted. Missiles, or kidneys, or whatever. So I'm sorry, because this kind of money, in this kind of way, might end up being annoying to you, you see, because they'll always know where it is, and they'll always want to tell you what to do with it."

If I had all that cash now I'd probably bury most of it in the yard to keep it safe.

"What for?" the man asks when I tell him I need change. He eyes me oddly and fingers his name tag. I point to the coin game, and he nods. He takes my dollar, presses a button on the register and hands me four quarters from the drawer that springs open. Before I even walk away from the counter the woman behind me asks for a pack of Marlboro cigarettes.

The floor in front of the game is sticky from spilled soda. It's a simple game really. You drop your quarter in a slot and guide it to land on a metal platform that is lined with other quarters. Then, a metal wall, about three inches tall, comes and pushes all the quarters forward toward a little cliff, and all the quarters that fall off the cliff drop into a bin and you get to keep them.

I drop the first quarter in. There are so many eagles and George Washingtons looking up at me. I aim toward the right side of the platform, where a cluster of quarters seems poised to be pushed off. My quarter lands and takes a little bounce. The wall comes out. It nudges two quarters to the edge of the platform, but nothing falls. I drop another quarter and aim it toward the same side, and this time the bounce looks perfect, but when the wall pushes, again nothing drops. There are four quarters hanging over the lip of the wall when I drop the third quarter, and again I aim at the right side, and again nothing drops. So, I smack the side of the machine, the side where the five quarters are dangling, and the man at the register clears his throat, and I look over at him. "Problem?" he asks. "No problem," I say. I take the fourth quarter and put it half way into the slot. I think for a second, and decide not to drop it.

Judith used to whisper questions to me too. Once she pulled me toward her, "Psst," she said, "what do you think the moon is made of?" We were on a walk through the neighborhood. A walk we used to take all the time. We'd cut through all the streets and come out in a shopping center that had a fountain in the middle of it, and Judith would whisper me questions and we'd drop coins in the fountain and then tell each other our wishes. We don't make that walk anymore. Last time we went was during winter, and the fountain was empty, and Judith dropped a coin in it, and it bounced around at the bottom, and I asked, "What did you wish for?" but she didn't tell me. She just looked at me and ran her hand through her hair.

In the treatment there wasn't much I could do. I invented a game where I had to drink as much water as I could. I had a little Dixie cup, and I'd stand in front of the sink in the bathroom and stare at the blank wall in front of me where the mirror had been, and I'd pretend that people would come from all over to challenge me to see if they could drink more water, and I'd fill up my little Dixie cup and take a shot, and then I'd fill it up and take a shot, and fill it up and shoot it, and take a shot, and another shot, all the while just leaving the water running, so I could just pass the cup through the stream of water and then take a shot, and pass through the stream and take a shot, and I'd do that until when I jumped I heard bubbles in my belly, unless the competition was really fierce. If the competition was fierce I would do it until the water came back up out of me.

   I don't even read the paper, which is why it's such a good idea. I've seen people selling papers on the corner, and so I know that there's a few ways to do it well. The first way is to have a funny hat. People are always buying papers from folks with funny hats, but the problem is I left mine at home in the closet. It would have been a good one too. Judith and I had bought matching hats that we wore to a Halloween party, and they both had tons of colors, like a jester's, and they had bells on the tops that jingled. The other way you can sell papers is if you're handicapped. Folks with one leg, for instance, they sell stacks and stacks of papers no problem because of the guilt. I got a bit of finger missing, but I don't think folks would be able to see that from their car windows. The last way is to dance, and I'm an excellent dancer. You don't have to know any steps really, you just have to move around a bit. There doesn't even need to be any music. You just have to feel it from inside.
   I found a paper dispenser that was totally full, and I slid in my quarter and I got every paper out from inside. Then I went to the busiest corner I could think of and I stood there by my stack of papers dancing. And, when the light went red, I'd go out between the cars and dance with a paper in my hands. I'd shuck my shoulders, and roll my tummy, and just stare at the people through their

windows. That's part of it. Persistence. Some people walk around to a bunch of different cars trying to play the averages, thinking someone in a slew of stopped cars is going to want to buy themselves a paper and read the news, but not me. I pick like two cars over the span of one red light. I go straight up to the driver's side window, hold up my paper, stare into their eyes and dance at them. Most everyone I did that to bought a paper. They might have laughed at me a bit, or looked away for a spell, but they sure as shit bought papers. It only took like twenty red lights before my stack was totally gone, and I made six dollars and a quarter.

One time the lawn mower went backwards too. That was the last time I mowed the lawn. I was going in straight lines, not missing a blade of grass, and then I just heard it change directions, and I guess it didn't matter too much, because the grass was still getting cut, but it bothered my ears so I leaned it back. I took my hand off the throttle, and when I did it died, and so I restarted the mower, but it was still going backwards, and so I leaned it back again, but this time I kept my foot on the throttle. I peered around the side of the mower, and sure enough the blade was spinning wrong, but it didn't seem too fast to fix, and I just knew that if I got it the right way, if I touched it just certain, that I could pause the blade and correct it, and I could finish the lawn no problem. Judith must have thought it was a bad idea what I was doing, because she came running out into the backyard screaming, and it was her screaming that distanced me, or maybe I chanced it too quick, so that she'd be proud that I fixed it, because I just smiled and said, "Got it," and then I drove my finger at the rusty spinning blade, but something so wrong happened, because I heard a sound like a bell chime, and my foot, by itself, just came off the throttle, and then my favorite finger, empty at the end, nothing but blood in the place the nail used to be. And then blood down my forearm. And then blood on Judith.

I'm so good at the lottery, and I didn't even know it. I bought six scratch off tickets, and rubbed them all clean with my last quarter while standing at the convenience store counter and I made two hundred dollars. The guy behind the counter didn't believe me when I told him. He looked at the ticket a dozen times while I blew all the lottery ticket dust to the floor. He had to call his manager, or something, but when he hung up the phone he came back to the register and pressed a button, and the drawer came out and he counted me out five twenties and gave me a hundred dollar bill. I touched all of the bills twice before putting them into my pocket, and then I walked up and down the aisles, but I didn't want to buy anything they had. But then, when I was leaving, I passed a gum ball machine, and I tossed in my quarter, and twisted the knob, and a blue ball fell into my hand. I popped it in my mouth and chewed it until it became soft. When it was soft I blew a bubble. The biggest bubble I'd ever blown, maybe the size of a coconut. I wished I'd had a camera. The man behind the counter saw, and he must have been jealous, because he rolled his eyes at me. I didn't mind much, because I was proud. When the bubble popped the gum stuck to my face. Then I left the store.

It feels good to have a pocket of money. That's all I can think about as I walk across the parking lot and toward the street. I can't remember the last time I had money of my own. I usually have to ask Judith to buy me things.

There's a parked car in the parking lot, and the trunk is open and there's a man with miniature Schnauzers for sale, and they're black and brown, and they look like the military, except their faces are cuter, and all their tails wag. The man smiles at me when I stop and bend over to pet them. I pick one up. It wriggles in my hand and licks at its nose.

"How much you asking?" I ask the man. He smiles. He's missing some teeth, but it's hard to tell which ones, because the ones that he does have are sort of buckled over each other and brown.

"Two fifty," he says. He has some type of accent that I've never heard before.

I cradle the puppy in one arm and take all of the money from my pocket with my free hand. I blow a bubble and hand the man the wad of bills. He counts it twice and frowns. Then he counts it a third time and nods his head. I think this means we have a deal. "Yes?" I say.

"Yes," he says.

He sort of shrugs and pats the dog on the head for the last time and I walk across the parking lot petting the puppy and blowing bubbles, and in the sky there's a plane and I start to think about Judith. I wonder if it's her plane. I wonder if she's sitting first class. I hope she has a safe trip to Florida. I hope she brings me back a present.

TUXEDOS

That was a special night. I dressed my testicles in matching tuxedos.

We went to a slick night club after the premier. The movie was in black and white. It was a homosexual adaptation of Macbeth and all the actors smoked cigarettes.

Under court orders I had quit drinking. I ordered an ice water at the after party. It came in a martini glass. Everyone assumed I was drinking. They began to whisper.

I drank my water slowly. I did not lose control. I felt cool and clean when the music began. I ordered more water.

I walked onto the dance floor. I do not dance. A thin blonde German in a pencil skirt moved toward me.

"Dance with me." She had a sticky accent.

I began to move. I'm no good at dancing. I bounced my shoulders front and back. I bent at the hip. I looked a loose-screwed robotica.

She laughed.

The music pumped like fists of heat. The German's sex parts dragged my knee.

I became rather hot. I finished my drink.

She touched my nose and walked to the bar.

She came back a minute or two later. She was drinking something pink. She had brought me a real martini.

I sipped it. My eyes swung open like push-button umbrellas.

"Something wrong?" she asked.

"No," I said.

We danced. Intermittently I sipped my drink. Cold, salty and tight. Fancy as a bowtie.

It happened quickly.

"What are you thinking about?" she asked.

"About something fantastic."

"Tell me," she said. We grinded to the music.

"I'll do better than that," I said. "I can show you."

"How exciting," she said. "Germans love to see things."

I set down the martini glass as the music grumbled on.

I unzipped my pants.

"Oh, dear," she said. Her face went flush.

"Wait, wait," I told her, and then I pulled out my scrotum.

Her mouth dropped open and she screamed. She slapped my face.

I looked down. I couldn't blame her. Somehow the tuxedos were gone. So was the German. Disappeared in the dancing crowd. The music came to a halt, but the strobe lights pulsed on. The other dancers froze like scarecrows. My pants bunched at my ankles.

"Are they in my sox?" I screamed. I didn't understand it. I felt so revealed. "Could they have fallen in my sox?"

The crowd parted, and I was left there alone. Sipping my martini. My lower half naked. My testicles jostled when the bouncers grabbed me.

GERMS FROM BLOOD

Trevor picks a crystal of salt off a pretzel and sets it on his tongue. It dissolves as he clicks his teeth. He drums his fingers on the table and taps his feet on the floor. His face is oily. His jeans are stained. He takes a sip of soda and slurps it, his mouth half open. He swallows. He whistles. He pats his thighs. He takes a mustard packet from the table and opens it with his teeth. He squirts a mound of mustard onto a napkin. He pulls a piece of pretzel from the knot and mashes it into the yellow clot. He chews the dough. He swallows. He takes another mustard packet and again opens it with his teeth.

"Aren't you worried?" Winston asks wide eyed.

"Bout what?"

"Germs?"

Winston's legs are crossed and he's holding a bottle of water. Trevor looks at the table. He looks at his hands.

"What germs?"

"The mustard." Winston points to the empty packets.

"I just opened them."

"With your teeth."

"Yeah, my teeth, so what?" Trevor takes another piece of pretzel and dips it in the mustard.

"So what?" He points to a man behind the counter. A hefty-lipped slacker with a zit the size of a dime on his chin. "That's the guy who put those mustards out. Touched them with his hands."

Winston and Trevor watch the man behind the

counter. He squeezes his lower lip with the thumb and forefinger of his right hand. He breathes deep through his nostrils, and his glasses rise on his face. Trevor picks up one of the empty mustard packets and puts the whole thing in his mouth. He chews it like gum and spits it on the table.

"So fucking what?" he says.

Winston takes a sip of his water. He clears his throat and looks at the packet that lays chewed on the table covered with spit.

"Disgusting," Winston says.

"Shit," says Trevor. "You should have seen what I was doing with my mouth last night."

Winston's back is to the door. Trevor has mustard on his chin. The woman they're to kill is somewhere in the store.

"What do you think she did?" asks Trevor.

Winston whispers, "I don't give a fuck." He takes a piece of paper from his shirt pocket.

"She's pretty," Trevor says.

"I thought you were into boys."

"Even so, you still know pretty when you see it." Trevor wipes his face with a napkin.

"Yeah, she's pretty," Winston agrees. He has taken a pen from behind his ear and begins drawing cubes on the paper. Trevor watches him.

"How long we known each other?" Trevor asks.

The muscles in Winston's face go slack. He stops drawing and taps the butt of the pen against the table. "Four years," he says.

Trevor takes a sip of soda. "Exactly," he says. "Four years."

Winston blinks. He begins again to draw. "If you knew why'd you ask?"

"I'm making a point."

"What's the point?"

"Well for four years, Chavez been pawning me off on you. . ."

"Don't say his name."

Heming way

"Sorry. . ."

"It's fucking amateur."

"Sorry." Trevor rolls his eyes. "Anyway," he continues, "for four years boss been pawning me off on you, and for four years, at every fucking job, you pull out your God damn pen, and start doodling your little fucking ice cubes, and I don't get it."

"There's nothing to get."

"You got some kind of fetish?"

"No."

"You got the autism, like Rainman?"

"No."

"Then what's the deal?"

Winston puts his pen behind his ear. "They're not ice cubes."

"What are they?"

"Cubes."

"Cubes of what?"

"Cubes of nothing. They're geometric shapes."

"I know what a cube is."

"Then why'd you ask?"

"Cause I'm trying to figure it out."

"Figure out what?"

"Surely you must realize that it's odd for a grown man to doodle cubes on scrap paper in public for four years."

Winston laughs. "I suppose."

"So?"

"Do you like music?" Winston asks.

"What?"

"Music."

"What the fuck does music have to do with cubes?"

"Nothing."

"Then what the hell are you talking about?"

"I'm getting to it."

"Getting to what?"

Winston flexes his jaw. "Just answer the question, you dirty little fag."

"What question?"

Winston's hand comes down against the table top with a crack. An old Mexican man in a pink guayabera gets up from a nearby seat. He walks away shaking his head.

"Do you like fucking music?"

"No God damn it."

"No?" Winston looks puzzled. He leans back in his chair. He puts his hands behind his head. "Who doesn't like music?"

"Me."

Winston bites his lower lip. "Well, then," says Winston. "What is it that you like?"

"Football," says Trevor.

"Football," says Winston. He smiles. He nods his head. "Do you follow any particular team?"

"Not anymore," says Trevor. "Used to the Houston Oilers, but now I just watch whatever's on."

"The Oilers," says Winston. "Warren Moon?"

"Yeah," says Trevor. "Warren Moon."

Winston laughs. "Well," he says. "What was Warren Moon most famous for?"

"Aside from being black?" says Trevor.

"Yes," says Winston. "What was the best part of his game?"

"Spirals," says Trevor. He moves his arm in a passing motion. "He threw long, pretty passes."

Winston nods his head. "Fine," he says. "And how do you think he got to be such a pretty passer?"

Trevor's eyes follow a phantom path. "Practice."

"Exactly," says Winston. "Controlled, disciplined practice." Winston smiles. He traces a scratch on the table with his finger. It is quiet, save for the laughter of a young girl climbing on a shopping cart.

Trevor looks puzzled.

"You draw cubes to learn football?" he asks.

Winston's eyes bulge. "No."

"Huh," says Trevor. "Well no offense, but I'm further away from understanding. I always just figured you were a touch crazy, but now I'm getting the feeling it's full blown."

The woman to be killed is at the back of a long line of customers funneling toward a check out. Winston watches her. "Art," he says, without looking at Trevor. "I'm practicing art."

Trevor laughs. "You a painter or something?"

"Yeah," Winston says. "Something."

Winston and Trevor watch the woman laying her groceries on the counter. She has long brown hair and tanned skin. She moves gently. She smiles at the cashier. She speaks to him. "How's it going?" Her voice floats across the room.

"Who's going to do it?" asks Winston.

"Doesn't make much difference."

"It makes a lot of difference."

"Why?"

"So we know procedure."

"Do you want to?"

"Doesn't matter what I want," says Winston. "What did boss tell you?"

"He didn't."

"Shit."

"Should we call him?"

"Do you have his number?"

"No, thought maybe you did."

"Uh uh. When he needs me he calls from a private line."

"Same."

"Who did the last one?"

"Last what?"

"What do you think?"

"No, I mean, last job, or, last job together?"

"Don't know. Didn't realize you worked with anyone else."

"Did a chef with that Rastafarian called Knuckles last Tuesday."

"I did a stewardess the same day solo."

"How'd you do it?"

"Doesn't matter."

"We made it look like the guy slipped and fell on his knife." Trevor simulates a falling motion, then smiles.

Winston shakes his head. "Who was the man on the last job we did together?"

"Can't remember."

"Think."

"Well what was it."

"The job? I think that was the junkyard guy. He was under a hood. We brought it down on him."

"I remember. There was that leashed dog that kept barking."

Both men are quiet.

"Flip a coin?" Trevor asks.

"Rather not," Says Winston. His water bottle is empty. He takes the pen from behind his ear and again draws cubes.

"What was the time before that?"

Winston frowns and places the paper and pen in his pocket. "Bartender. I pushed him down the basement stairs. He was carrying a case of Bud."

"Oh, yeah," Trevor says nodding. "Guess it's my turn then."

The two men stand and walk toward the automatic-door exit. One man positioned on either side. Winston grabs a Pennysaver from a rack and looks at the cover page. Trevor drops a quarter into a prize-redemption game and moves a dangling claw with a joystick over a reservoir of stuffed animals. Trevor pushes a red button. The claw drops into the pile. Its flimsy aluminum fingers slip across the back of a fuzzy, pink hippopotamus dressed in a blue tuxedo. The animal shifts. The claw catches the corner of the animal's jacket. It retracts and the hippo rises. The momentum from the shift carries and the animal swings on a pivot as the claw ascends.

Trevor holds his breath. He moves the joystick gently, and the claw rides on a track towards a bin. Trevor presses the red button again and the doll falls.

"I didn't think that was possible," a woman says.

Trevor pulls the hippo from a bank which is covered by a swinging door. The door flutters on its plastic hinges.

"Me either," Trevor says. He turns. It's their woman. She has a wide bright smile, and her head is tilted. Trevor flashes a silly grin. There is mustard on his face. He offers the woman the doll by shoving it in her direction. "Want it? I don't much care for stuffed animals."

"Then why'd you play?" the woman asks. She laughs and brushes past Trevor on her way out the door.

Winston drops the Pennysaver and walks to Trevor. They watch the woman. "Smooth," says Winston.

Trevor throws the stuffed animal toward a trash can. He misses. They walk out into the sun. Winston takes a pair of sunglasses from his pocket and slips them on. Trevor squints his eyes. They follow the woman on foot through the shady streets. They linger behind tree trunks and at corners so she doesn't see. Four blocks north. Two blocks east. There they take a seat on a wooden bench and watch the woman climb a flight of stairs to her apartment. The streets are quiet save an occasional car.

Winston looks at his watch. Trevor watches her apartment door.

"Do you like this job?" Trevor asks Winston.

Winston looks at him. He looks across the street. "Nerves?"

"Nah."

"Emotions?"

"Uh uh."

"What?"

Trevor rubs his palms together. He keeps his eyes on the apartment. "The art is all," he says.

"Oh," says Winston. "A hobby."

Trevor looks at Winston's hands. Winston is wearing a pair of black-leather gloves.

"I thought I was doing it," Trevor says.

"You are," says Winston. "I'm just particular about what I touch."

Trevor laughs. His teeth are yellow. His laughter fades.

"What's so funny?" asks Winston.

Trevor looks at his hands. "Would you rather be doing art?" Trevor asks.

"Then what?"

"Then this."

"Maybe," says Winston. "I'm not sure."

Trevor shows his hands to Winston. He puts them close to his face, and Winston leans back. "In a few minutes I'm gonna go across that street, and climb them stairs and kill that woman," Trevor says. "With these." Trevor moves his hands closer to Winston's face, and Winston moves further back. "And when I'm doing it, there won't be anywhere I'd rather be."

"Good for you," Winston says.

"It is good," says Trevor. "I'm exactly what I want to be."

Winston nods his head. A black Lincoln drives slowly by. Both men watch it pass.

"It's a good enough job," says Winston.

Trevor snorts.

"What?" asks Winston.

The door to the apartment opens slightly, then closes. An orange tabby cat springs down the stairs and through the yard adjacent the complex.

"You still engaged?" asks Trevor.

"I am," says Winston.

Trevor spits on the ground. "And how much money did you clear last year?" Trevor asks.

"About sixty thousand," Winston says.

Trevor nods. "Not bad."

"It's a living."

"What do you tell her?"

"What do you mean?"

"When you bring home the money, without going to work. You draw a pretty decent cube, but I'm sure you can't convince her that you sell those scraps of paper."

Winston laughs. "No, she knows I haven't made money off it yet."

"So what does she think?"

Winston touches his face with his black gloves. He breathes deep. "She thinks I sell insurance," he says.

A woman with a stroller walks down the sidewalk past the men. Trevor nods his head at her, and she smiles. Then he looks at Winston. "What like life insurance?"

Both men laugh.

"Jesus, no," says Winston. "Bankruptcy."

"Wait," Trevor says, "wouldn't you make more?"

"Nope," he says. "I'm no good at it, but she understands."

"How so?"

"She says I'm not suited."

"Why?"

"On account of the art," says Winston. "She says artist can't be salesman."

Trevor nods and Winston looks away. The street is still.

"You ready?" Trevor asks.

"For what," asks Winston. "I'm just along for the show."

Trevor makes to stand, but the Lincoln is back and moving slower.

"Same one as earlier," Trevor says.

"Maybe we should sit tight a bit."

Trevor takes a menthol cigarette from his pocket and places it in his lips. He lights it and inhales deeply. He blows smoke toward the street. Winston rubs his thumbs against his forefingers. The leather gloves squeak.

"What about you?" asks Winston.

"What about what?" says Trevor.

"You with anyone?"

"Oh," says Trevor. "No, I don't do that."

"Do what?"

"Stay with someone," says Trevor. "I keep things casual."

"I see," says Winston.

"It gets lonely," says Trevor, "but it's worth it."

"Uh huh."

"I mean there was a fella once," says Trevor. "But it didn't work out."

"Why?"

"I told him what I do," Trevor says.

"What you *do*, do?" asks Winston.

"Yep," says Trevor.

"How'd he take it?"

"Not well."

"What happened?"

Trevor drops his cigarette on the cement and mashes it with his heel. He looks at Winston. "We're not together anymore," Trevor says.

Winston nods.

"Listen," says Trevor. "I think that car was coincidence, and I don't really feel like waiting around any longer."

"Okay," says Winston. "You make the call."

Trevor nods. He stands and walks. Winston follows him across the street and through the yard. They climb the stairs slowly. The soles of their shoes scrape gently against the cement steps. They come to the door, and Trevor raises his fist. He brings his knuckles down swiftly, so there is one solid knock. Trevor lets his hands fall to his sides. The door opens. The woman smiles. There is confusion in the corners of her eyes.

"Hey you're the guy. . . ."

Trevor grabs her throat with his left hand, and places his right hand over her mouth. He drives her back into the apartment. She screams, but it is muffled. Winston steps across the threshold and closes the door behind him. Trevor and the woman land on the floor. He grinds his weight against her throat. She kicks her feet against the floor and scratches at Trevor's back. She screams into his hand, and Trevor shushes her.

"Calm down sweetheart," Winston says. He sits on the sofa and begins to leaf through a magazine.

There is one last thud of a heel against the hardwood. Then silence.

"She done?" Winston asks.

Trevor sits back. "Done."

Winston sets the magazine down. He stands and heads for the door. "You coming?" he asks Trevor. Winston looks back. Trevor has not moved. His shoulders are rocking. "You okay?" he asks.

Trevor looks up. His lips are stretched tightly into a smile. "How much you wanna bet she thought it was over the animal?"

"What animal?"

"The stuffed animal at the store?"

"How you figure?"

"I don't know," Trevor says. "Like she probably thought I killed her because she didn't take it. Probably wished she had the whole time."

"Doesn't matter," Winston says.

"It does to her."

Trevor looks at the woman's eyes. They are open and blood shot. His hand is still on her face.

"You ready?" asks Winston.

Trevor shrugs. "Remember the man I told you about?" Trevor asks.

"Which one?" asks Winston.

"The one I was with."

"Yeah."

"The one that I told."

"I remember."

"He was a special education teacher. Not a teacher really. An assistant is what he called himself. And when I told him he kind of lost it, talking about making a difference and making a change."

"Okay."

"But we do make changes," Trevor says. "This is a change." He nods at the woman who lies dead on the hardwood beneath him. He looks at Winston. "And no matter what that guy did his kids were still going to be retarded," Trevor says. He laughs. He looks down at his hands.

"I suppose so," Winston says.

"Hey," says Trevor. He looks at his finger. "Can you get germs from blood?"

"What," Winston says.

Trevor holds up his finger. The tip is dark red. "Must've squeezed her mouth too hard," he says.

Winston shakes his head. "Wash it off."

Trevor stands. There is sinister in his eyes. He moves slowly toward Winston with his finger stretched long and aimed for him.

"What are you doing?" asks Winston.

Trevor stabs with his finger, and Winston moves back.

"Stop it God damn it." Winston's lips quiver as he walks backward away from the blood.

Trevor laughs. He picks up speed. Winston turns. Trevor chases him around the coffee table and in circles through the living room. They both jump over the torso of the dead woman. Their feet leave scuff marks on the hardwood.

"Stop it you dirty little faggot."

Trevor's laugh is high and shrill. "It's just a little blood," he says. "I'm gonna dab it on your nose."

Winston lunges up on the sofa. He turns quickly and draws his gun. He forces the barrel at Trevor's face. "Knock it the fuck off," he says.

Trevor smiles. He rocks his head from side to side. "What," he says. "Just having some fun."

"Yeah, well fun's over." Winston pulls the hammer of the revolver back with his thumb.

"Gonna shoot me," Trevor asks.

"Wash it off."

"Wash what off?"

Winston motions with the gun toward the blood. "The finger," Winston says.

"Oh this," Trevor says. He brings the finger between them. A bead of blood rolls toward his palm.

"Yes," says Winston. "That." He steps down off the sofa but keeps the gun aimed at Trevor.

"Shit," says Trevor. "Only fooling." He shrugs and leans his head to one side. He brings his hand up to his face and laughs. His eyes are locked with Winston's. Winston's face is calm. Trevor puts the finger into his mouth and draws it out slowly across his tightened lips. He smiles. He swallows. Then Winston puts away the gun.

WATER-FILLED JUGS

Drywall catches fire at four hundred fifty one degrees. I live between a checkpoint and a border. South ten miles and across a river, the wild Mexican state of Frontera Tamaulipas. North fifty miles, the town of Falfurrias, Texas where police dogs sniff cars for illegals and narcotics, their wet noses shiny as freshly minted change. August and the temperature is a hundred fifteen. In the field behind my house the cacti parch, their skins paling in the sun, their needles a vivid yellow against the backdrop of anemic sky. It could get hotter. Thin wisps of clouds like strands of smoke haunt the horizon, and flames swill across the perimeter of the sun. I'm near a quarter way there. I can hear the birds singing.

My wife lies with her belly to the cool tile in the other room. Her blonde hair glued by sweat to her brow. In another room still the siren of my daughter's discontent emits. Braised wails rake like a shovel's blade against a grind stone spinning. There is a weight when the panic strikes. Directions need changing, but the temperature holds steady and the drywall remains unfazed beneath coats of paint. Could I force it open with a window? Could flames swim through like a river's current raging?

The tap water here is stringent and the radio speaks another language. We walk home from a filtration center carrying water-filled jugs beneath a parasol. My daughter sleeps in a stroller with the canopy drawn. Those who pass in cars with raised windows look upon us with their tinted faces frowning as though we're chancing something sinister—spitting on the pages of a bible, sleeping with the lights on. The jug water evaporates before we arrive home, but we refill them from the faucet and pretend the journey worth it. No smiles stretch while we're pretending. We watch the walls with thirsty tongues unquenched.

In the evening we hear the toy shaped music of the ice-cream man's cart, but we've yet to see him. We stand beneath Spanish Olive trees counting the white blossoms as they fall to the dirt. My wife collects them once they've landed. She wishes she could braid them into a blanket for the baby. I wish the ice-cream man would walk his cart toward us, tip his hat and take our money into his vanilla-scented hands. Then the cheap preached tune of the cart dries to a quiet cluck. It tapers off completely as the sun sets.

A dear friend sent us the skeleton of a man. It came in a cedar box with a schematic for assembling. It stands now in the center of our home, and my wife draws upon it with crayons. She draws flowers and butterflies and smiling faces across its skull and ribs. She says the pictures will soothe the baby. The baby cries while my wife does the drawing. My wife pauses to sniff the cedar-scented skeleton. She takes its hand into her hands.

At night in the field with my leather satchel searching. The moon pale as a patient on oxygen. In the distance coyotes wail. My naked hands powdered by the pears' fine needles. I make for home once the satchel's heavy. The silhouette of the house is little more than a mystery to my eyes when the baby's cries bring ache to my ears. I empty the satchel. The pears drum the ground. I tread back out into the deadly field, zigzagging from cactus to cactus until my satchel's filled again.

Beneath the parasol carrying jug water:
Wife: Is it worth it?
Me: What?
Wife: The future. It feels fixed as seasons. It's all just chapters stationed in wait, patterned out by the families that have come before. Did I tell you I've taken up crocheting? You should have a hobby.
Me: I thought your hobby was drawing on the skeleton for the baby.
Wife: It was. I covered the bones with drawings of flowers and smiles, and the baby cried, so I covered the bones with drawings that made them look like plain bones, and the baby cried, so I covered the bones back with flowers and smiles, but none of the drawings changed any of the things. Do you ever pay attention?
Me: Listen.
From behind a fence a conversation. A language I'd never known. My wife and I press our eyes to the cracks between boards, and a man in a linen suit holds a sword to the throat of a woman who sits naked on a stool. Then the man leans forward and drains her blood with his blade, slow out the jugular, the crimson thumping out in heaves, and she slumps from the stool to the canary-colored grass gasping, and the man wipes his blade clean with a handkerchief from his breast pocket.
Wife: That poor woman.
Me: Maybe she had it coming.

*   *   *

In the front lawn in a chair I sit with crossed legs and a boy across the street tosses a ball onto the roof of his house. The ball rolls down the pitch of the roof and lands in his outstretched hands. My wife lies in the grass on her side sipping water from a straw as the baby nurses. I thumb the treads of my sneakers and dirt drops through the stale air.

The baby is shrill and the wife stands above me. The lamp is lit and the room glows with nauseous light.
Wife: The skull is gone.
Me: What?

I run through the streets with my hand extended. I've spotted his shadow, and the shadow of his cart, and I hear the music clucking louder than ever. It haunts me like a fever and sweat slicks my skin. His image quivers in the syrupy mirages swimming across the surface of the black asphalt that separates us. I quicken my pace, but I can't seem to gain. His outline harasses the horizon like the flame of a candle being cinched from my vision as though robbed slowly of air. He fades away entirely as my lungs start to throb. Lost in the chasm of endless bending light. His music follows shortly after. Once I can't hear it I slow to a stride.

Drywall is made of gypsum plaster encased in paper. I hold a magnifying glass between it and the sunlight that rains through the window. The light narrows to a tiny bead, and smoke slips from the spot it hits. It smells like the Fourth of July, but the earth moves and the sun's rays fade from the window before I can get a good blaze going.

The boy pitches to the roof top and the ball grinds back toward him, thumping the shingles as it moves back to its source. I'm almost asleep. My hat hides my eyes in shadow and my body prays for a breeze. Then my wife tugs my pant leg.

Wife: What's that he's throwing?

The boy lobs again. The thrown thing strikes the roof and rolls unevenly back toward him. I stand, my eyes on his hands, and cross the street.

"Boy," I say to him, but he doesn't respond. "Boy."

He catches the skull and looks back at me.

"Where'd you get that?" I ask. The boy shrugs his shoulders, and I hold out my hand. "Give it on back," I tell him, but he pulls it behind him and shakes his head no. "Don't make me tell your father," I say. I hold my finger at his face and the front door to his house opens.

"Can I help you?" a wide-shouldered man calls as he steps out on the lawn.

"Your boy's got my skull," I tell him.

He looks at me with a glazed face, "Excuse me," he says.

I point to the boy. "In his hand," I tell him.

The man touches his son's shoulder and raises his chin to the boy, "What you got?"

The boy pulls his hand from behind his body and raises the skull, covered with flowers and butterflies, at his father. "My skull," says the boy. "I've always had it."

The father shakes his head and pats the boy. "It's *his* skull," he says and looks up at me. "He's *always* had it."

"He's lying," my wife calls out from across the street.

128

I raise my palm toward my wife and stomp my foot on the dirt. I look at the father, who's now grinding his teeth. "He's lying," I tell him.

The father nods. "Prove it."

I point to the skull. "The flowers," I say, "on the skull," I nod, "my wife drew those."

The man takes the skull from his son and looks at it through thinned eyes. He licks his thumb and runs it across one of the flowers, and the flower disappears as his thumb grows stained. "What flowers?" he says.

Me: But I do have a hobby.

My wife takes a pear from the stack and drops it into the boiling water, counts to ten, and fishes it out with a spider skimmer and drops it into a bath of ice water, and the flesh goes a bloody plum color. I hold the baby, and she cries, and her face draws the blood from her body and her cheeks change hue until they match her lips and gums, and her toothless mouth stretches wide, and her lips tense like fists, and I rub her face gently into mine, but it doesn't quell her fury, and her mother looks at me, and strikes the spider against the pot, and asks me why I'm so bad at it.

"Bad at what?" I ask her.

"Bad at everything," she says.

The coyotes run in packs of six, and I am not afraid of them. I chased them across the plane in the moonlight dodging cactus paddles. Their sandy colored bodies flittered down narrow paths. My legs took messes of needles and my satchel swung wildly about me. I could hear their calls ahead of me as I sprinted through the thicket of mesquite.

The moon made shine the needles abounding. I trailed them north toward the freeway, and the horizon ahead of us glowed, and I could hear the hum of the cars traveling. The coyotes turned to parallel the road about a mile off from it, and we made our way south toward the rail road tracks, shucking through the paddles, and thorns, and brush, and sand, and my shoes filled with pebbles, and their shadowy bodies flittered in and out of the light cast by the moon, and they fanned about like thread of a loom weaving, but I stayed behind the center coyote running, and even though they'd make off the course by dozens of yards they'd converge briefly before fanning out again, barking and yelping high pitched squeals as I'd near them. In the distance the train running. Its machine hiss and grind coasting the tracks. It blew its steam horn, and the lead coyote piqued his head and gathered speed. I sped up too. My blood raced inside me and my throat and lungs heavied. They came together in a tight squadron moving south as the train cut the plane heading west. They picked their spot and raced toward it and I followed some ten yards behind them. The train thumped against the track and the light from the locomotive made weak the moon light, and the patch of wilderness west of us lit up, but the ground around my feet seemed to darken. The six coyotes drew into two lines. I stayed centered behind them. The train gunned toward the spot we aimed for, and threw two quick blasts of the horn. It trailed deep into the eastern distance, so little more than shadows of the subsequent cars could be made out by the eyes. We raced on, the train raced on, the coyotes lowered their heads and the lead dog pulled away, and the two lines came together as one, and their paws pumped beneath their bodies and landed near silently against the thin-grassed ground, and the train wake grew heavy in our chests, and its squealing wheels against the tracks burnt our ears, and it slowed the coyotes for fear, and then I was upon them, a half step from the trail of the pack, and then I was with them, running up the slope towards the track, and shadows in every direction and my heart and breath lost in the hiss of the engine. The train was less than a dozen yards from us, and I didn't look because I couldn't look, my eyes on the six ahead of me climbing, and then the horn again, and I swear I could taste it, and the coyotes yelped as they gained speed, the shadows, and the hollers, and the hill, and the horn, but it wasn't couldn't, sprinting, and my breaths whistled across my throat, and then I was a train too, but sprinting, up the hill to beat it, and nearing, and nearing, but no way, I couldn't, my body too heavy, and I tried stopping cold but stepped funny and stumbled and fell to the dirt, and my palms were torn open by rocks and thorns, and the last two coyotes trailed to the right, but the others went forward, and when I sat up the remaining coyotes had doubled back, and they were walking in circles a ways down from me, and I sat still and watched them, as they barked at the train grumbling by us, and on the other side I could hear muffled barks answering, and then the two on my side threw their heads toward the moon and howled, and then the others howled back, and I screamed. I screamed too. I screamed at the train grinding by. And then the two coyotes tilted their heads and stared at me.

"Have you seen this?"
"No."
"You don't even know what I'm asking," my wife says and points to the wall. There are dozens of burns in a straight path descending. I run my palm across them.

"Must be bugs," I tell her and shrug.

She clicks her teeth. "And what about these?" she says and raises a pair of my pants, which are covered with dirt and thorns. "Bugs too?"

I take the pants from her hands and contemplate them. "I don't think so," I tell her.

The skull has a red bow tied through its eyes. It sits on the front porch when we return with the jugs. The pictures, the flowers and smiles, have been rubbed clean, and the once smooth dome of the skull has been roughed up by shingles. My wife picks it up and holds it in her hands. I look across the street at the home of the boy. "I think the blinds moved," I say. Then the baby screams.

The exterminator scratches his chin.

"What kind of bugs?" my wife says.

The exterminator kneels down and leans near the wall. He rubs his thumb across the holes. "Do you think," he says and looks up at my wife, "I could have a glass of water?"

My wife smiles, pulls the baby high on her hip and nods. "Do you want ice?" she asks.

The exterminator grins. His gray teeth look dead in his mouth. "Just tepid," he tells her.

When my wife is gone the exterminator stands. He looks at me and clears his throat. He looks around the room. He spots my magnifying glass and takes it from the window ledge. He inspects me through it, and his eye goes giant in the glass, wrinkles crawl from the slit like webs of a spider, and the white of his eyeball is laced with red veins. He lowers the glass and thumps it to his palm. His hands are rough and the color of clay. "Tisk," he says and shakes his head.

"Shut up," I say, and he pockets the glass when we hear my wife's steps in the hall.

My wife comes back with the water, and hands it to the exterminator, "Well," she says.

"Fire ants," the exterminator says and winks at me.

"Fire ants," my wife says and nods. "Can you get rid of them?"

The exterminator chugs the water in three big gulps. He hands the empty glass back to my wife. He takes off his hat and slicks back his thinning hair. "Sure," he says. "But it's kind of expensive."

"Your lips."

"What about them?"

"They taste like ice cream."

"Don't be stupid," my wife says.

One night I met the man with the sword in the thicket of cactus. He was singing a song and swinging his blade through the cactus paddles and I was filling my satchel with pears. The moon light was heavy enough that we could see each other's faces and he smiled at me and asked, "How do you do?" His accent had a cologne to it.

"I'm fine," I said and plucked a pear from a paddle.

"You like those?" he asked.

"They're okay," I told him.

He swung his sword and paddles flipped through the air.

"What are you doing?" I asked him.

"Releasing tension," he told me. He swung his sword again and ribbons of green flesh fell in every direction. He pulled a kerchief from his shirt pocket, wiped the blade and sheathed his sword. "Have you seen the immigrants out here?"

"I've seen coyotes," I told him.

"Sure," he said and nodded. "They're always

around." He looked up at the moon and wiped his brow with the back side of his kerchief. "Come with me," he said.

I followed him out of the ring of cacti and down a path that weaved through a forest of mesquite. We ducked and crept through the waist-level limbs until we came to a clearing. In the center of the clearing was a table. On the table were jugs of water. They looked like ghosts in the moon light, and the man with the sword held a finger to his lips, and we dropped to our knees, resting our elbows against a knotty mesquite branch, and in a few moments we heard voices.

The man with the sword pointed toward the edge of the clearing, and a small band of people made way from the shadows toward the table. They spoke, but I couldn't understand them.

"They're worried," the man with the sword said as the group neared the jugs of water.

"About what?" I asked.

Then the lights came on, giant high beams aimed at the table, and the man with the sword sprang from the mesquite trees and unsheathed his sword and charged at the immigrants swinging his blade furiously at them, and I jumped to my feet and ran for home screaming.

My wife sits on the sofa crocheting a blanket and the baby sleeps on her lap. I can't catch my breath.

"What's wrong?" she asks.

"We're not going for water anymore," I tell her.

She sets down her needles and holds up the blanket. "What do you think?"

I nod. "What's it for?"

My wife shrugs her shoulders. "The baby, I guess."

*   *   *

"I see you found your skull," the neighbor says, and he points to the window where the skeleton stands looking out on the street.

"Yes," I say. "What made you give it back?"

The neighbor is washing his car and I'm sweaty and out of breath from chasing the ice-cream man. I couldn't catch him.

"I got to thinking about it," the neighbor says, "and I couldn't remember the boy having one. My wife tied the ribbon on it. She's also the one that gave your wife the ice cream."

"Ice cream," I say.

"Sure," he says. "I didn't want you getting the wrong idea."

"Wrong idea?"

"You know. A guy gives a man's wife ice cream," the neighbor smiles and shrugs, "could be taken the wrong way."

"Sure," I tell him and force a smile.

"Anyhow, the guy was around with his cart."

"Here?" I say and look up and down the road.

"Um," the neighbor says and looks up and down the road too. "Yeah, the other day."

I run my hand through my damp hair and nod. My jaw tenses and my skin goes hot.

The neighbor's eyes go thin. He drops a sponge into a bucket of water. "So, like I said, he was around and my wife got some ice cream from him and gave it to your wife and all."

I kick a rock that sits on the ground and it bites and bounces down the street. "Of course you did," I tell him. "Of course."

I can feel my wife's eyes on me.

"What are you doing," she asks. "Are the bugs back?"

I hold my empty fist raised between the window and the wall. The sunlight hits the back of my hand, and my fist's shadow lands on the wall heavy. "No," I say and look at her. "Why don't you go with me to look for the ice cream man anymore?"

She shakes her head, "What do you mean?" she asks.

"Ice cream," I say.

She pats her thighs, "I don't. . ." The baby's cries come in from the other room. She motions toward the baby. "I've got to. . ."

I return my gaze to the shadow on the wall. "Of course you do," I say. I know there are easier ways.

The wind shucks the hat from my head, and I watch it disappear into the mess of mesquite branches. There are two five-gallon jugs of water. I set each on the ground and place the skull on the table. It still has the ribbon tied through its eyes. I pick up one of the jugs and hoist it to my shoulder. I pick up the other jug and do the same, but it is harder as my balance sways. I struggle from the clearing to the brush with my shoulders burdened. I worm my way through the tree limbs and out to the cactus plain. In the distance I hear cars pass. I move south toward the railroad tracks. The hot air is sweet, and my throat dries with each breath. The jugs ache my joints, and I feel the blood in the muscles of my back boiling. It takes me twenty minutes of dragging my feet before I reach the tracks, and my shirt is soaked, and the world is slightly spinning. I set the jugs down on the middle of the track. They glisten in the steady sun. I walk off to sit in the grass. Far away a plume of smoke fills the sky with black. I know the train will be through eventually. I wait there patiently for something inevitable.

SLUG TRAIL

I

It's miserable shopping, when hungry and sad.

II

If the leprosy returns I'll hold them hostage with rot.

III

On a bus ride through Texas I woke next to a man who stared over me, through the window and out across the plains. The man was not beside me before I fell asleep. He was wearing a camouflage jacket, and his breath smelled of licorice. He had red murky eyes and white ashy skin.

"My father made all of it."

I looked out the window at the flat land streaming by.

"What, like God?"

The man rubbed his face and flecks of skin swirled in the air. "You're funny to me. I've met the black you." He smiled.

"The black me?"

"Yeah, everyone has one. A black them. I met yours in Savannah in a candy shop by the river. He threw me a warm taffy. He was you but in black."

The man waved at something out the window that I couldn't see.

"So, all black people have white thems running around?"

The man laughed. The laughter woke a sleeping baby. The baby cried and cried. "You see? You're funny."

"Thanks."

Then the man looked at the flooring beneath his seat. "Holy shit, holy fucking shit."

"What?"

He stomped his feet. He leaned in close. He put a finger to his lips.

"This bus leaves a slug trail."

IV

I'll pull the alarm and they'll run from fear of fire.

V

My fourth grade teacher had a tattoo of a woman on his forearm. He liked to flex his muscle and make it dance. He watched me as I watched it dancing.

VI

Most of them did not scream, but walked to the exits, looking up as the sirens called. A train of people, all headed for doors.

VII

"They could follow the slug trail back to the start of the bus."

VIII

With my rot I'll back them into corners.

IX

Then we sat in the parking lot. We wanted to go back in. There was no smoke. There were families and friends in bundles talking about the alarm. There were security guards on Segways maneuvering through the crowd. I sat on the asphalt. Indian style as the siren sang. Then a man, dark as a red-wine bottle, stood beside me where I sat. He lifted his shirt sleeve to show me his arm. There was a woman tattooed on it. He flexed and the woman danced. He watched as I watched it.

I smiled. "I've met the white you."

The man dropped his shirt sleeve and shook his head.

"Shit," he said. "If I had a dime for every time someone told me that."

FREE FRIED PIE

The past couple times I've been curbed, which shouldn't provoke me to fret so, except there's poison in the process when it goes awry. A muted confusion extends. They shake their heads no as though you've mouthed a dirty thing, and they don't even chance a glance at the manager's office to determine if he's looking. If they look then you've a decent hope, so long as they can pull it off, but when their eyes go ample, as though you've dropped your order on the cement, then you know you're working different venues, and you'd just as well raise your window and drive along.

My asking was never routine. It was a seldom request I'd make. A real man doesn't need free fried pie, but he feels more a man when he comes by it that way. That's probably why I ever came to chance the query, "Throw in a free fried pie?" Because it made you feel mighty when they grinned and stepped back casual to the fry tray, and came back nervously dropping a pie at your car and waving you on. Up until these past couple times I'd a profound success rate. Might be I was a sounder judge of character. I could always spot a pie dropper straight off. Something in how they held their mouths. A sort of flaccid smile. As if to say, "I'd rather not be here." But these last couple of ladies, they held their mouths like that, as though stamped glumly on, the mark of the pie dropper, but they didn't want any part of my adventure, and it made me feel shame.

I told my brother about it, and he grinned

at me, and patted a hand on my stomach, but I brushed that gesture aside. I'm a slender specimen. A thirty inch waste when in blue jeans. That's three inches less than when I graduated high school, but I don't think that's my doing. I'm no leaner than I was then, but it seems every so often sizes reconfigure. An inch is an inch, except in blue jeans. Then an inch is whatever gets folks to purchase. I've dropped an inch every five years since graduating, except when in suit pants. Suit pants I'm still a thirty three, but I'm not sure the distinction. I guess folks that wear suit pants like to know if they're growing, and folks that wear blue jeans just like to think they've stayed same.

I've a birthday coming up. I'll be thirty four years of age. Don't think I've not placed blame on my age as culprit for the lack of free pie. I've stood in front of the mirror to investigate the lines that crawl away from my eyes, but they are slight in definition, and, from a distance more than arms length, cannot easily be identified, and so I don't blame them. Likewise with my hair. It's not begun to thin, and it's not begun to gray, and I've got magazines that show boys half my age with the same style. I've even put the blunt question toward a girl working the drive through window. I was stretching for the bag she was stretching to hand me, and I asked, "Do I look old?" And she laughed and told me, "No, sir," and then I chanced, "Throw in a free fried pie?" But she shook her head at me, and pulled tight her window, and I drove off with my window still down. I think it was a question too many. Folks seem to ration their positive answers these days.

For a while there I blamed the economy. The world's in a mess, what with the war and the job rate. My family's got mineral rights, so we've been unaffected for the most part. But I do have a nephew that went off to Iraq, and he came back wounded fiercely. Lost every limb except his left arm. There's not much he can do. He stays hunkered down on the sofa with the TV remote changing channels. He's a real ass hole about it too. Flips the station at crucial moments in the broadcasts. I haven't seen a touchdown or buzzer beater on the TV at my sister's house since he was released from the service. But if you ask the boy for the controller his mother looks at you as though you've asked for his last hand. I bet he could get free fried pie for days, but he won't leave his house ever. He says he forgets his wounds until he sees people looking. Other folk's eyes always reveal your weakness.

But they're still giving free pies, just not to me. I saw a youngster make a score at the Whataburger a few weeks back. He'd got his whole order, you could tell by the heft of it, and then, as the woman was retreating back into her window, he held a palm toward her, and then she held a finger at him. She came back in a flurry a moment later with a pie box in her hand, dropped it at him and waved toward the road. He drove off quick and I followed that son of a bitch. I trailed him to an apartment complex a couple miles down the way, and I parked before he got down and ran up to his window. "How'd you do it?" I asked him. And he threw a look of confusion, and I said, "The pie, God damn it, how'd you get it for free?" That boy, he laughed. He held the pie box at me. Said he, "Didn't even want it, just wanted to ask." He said, "You can have it, no problem, if you like." He smirked at me like I was missing limbs, and I snatched that pie from him, I did, but I didn't eat it. I drove around with it for a couple hours looking at the container. The orange and white box, and the cinnamon stench staining the air. Tried to pitch it a time or two, but couldn't bring myself to release it. Couldn't let it fall from my fingers. I still got it even. It's in the door of my freezer.

BABY GRAND DANGLE

Leroy hands me the shotgun and tells me to
kill him. "It's loaded," he says, and he closes his
eyes. He sits with his back to a window. Light
bathes his shoulders, and his bald scalp shines. He
puts his fingers to his forehead. "Aim for here,"
he says.

I wait a moment before I let the butt of the
gun slip from my hand. He hears the wooden stock
thump against the carpet. He opens his eyes and
stares at me.

"Don't be a pussy," he says. The muscles of his
wrinkled face pinch. His lips and cheeks bunch into
knots.

"Why do we do this every time?" I ask. I shake
my head and look at my corduroys. I thumb the
tufts above my knee. Leroy chews his bottom lip.

"Cause I'm in pain, Goddamn it." He leans
back in his chair. He puffs. His cheeks fill with
breath as his small shoulders sink.

I pick up the gun. I break the barrel and let
the shells fall to the floor. "Nope," I say. "Won't
happen."

"Come on, Connor. I'm falling apart. Yesterday
I shit myself. You ever shit yourself, boy?"

"Once," I tell him. "On a camping trip."

"On a camping trip," he says. He shakes his
head and leans forward. "Ever shit yourself on an
elevator? Full of people?"

"You didn't."

"Did," he says, and shifts in his chair. "I was

143

fine when I got on. Reached to push the button and it came grumbling out. Had to stare at the door the whole way up. Heard em snickering. Felt shit slurping around on the way back to my room."

I chuckle and rub my hands together. Leroy looks at me with blistering eyes.

"Sorry," I say. "I won't."

The room is hush. Leroy chews on the tip of his thumb. I look out the window behind him. We are sixteen floors up. There is a new building going up across the street. Cranes pull equipment into the air. Men wait with hooks to pull the equipment into the building.

"Bring the bourbon?"

"Sure," I say. I pull a brown bag from beneath my jacket. Leroy smiles.

"Good. Two fingers over ice and scram." He shakes his head. "I can't bear the look of you."

I nod and go to the kitchenette. I take a tumbler from a cabinet and fill it with ice. I pour the bourbon and the cubes pop and crack.

"You know," Leroy says. "You always were selfish." He looks at the shotgun as he speaks.

"How you figure?" I ask. I walk the drink to Leroy and set it in his hand.

"Your godfather was a barber," he tells me.

"So," I say.

"So, you always had long hair. You let it grow down over your ears like mess," he says. "It was insulting." Leroy takes a clove from a pack on the table. He lights it, takes a drag and fills the air with spiced smoke.

I clear my throat. "I wouldn't call it insulting."

"Really, what would you call it?"

"Nothing," I say and touch my head. "Besides, I keep it short now."

"Who cuts it?"

"Meredith," I tell him.

"Of course she does," he says. "She has to," he

rattles the ice in his glass. "Your godfather's been dead a half dozen years."

Meredith sits beside me at the table. I leaf through the newspaper, she's looking at a book. She moves in her seat. The chair legs squeak across the floor. I look at her.

"Sorry," she says.

I smile. I'm reading a story about the new building downtown. It's a hotel. There's going to be a jazz lounge on the top floor.

Meredith clears her throat. I look up from the page.

"Need some water?" I ask.

"No," she says. "We're fine."

She says *we* now. I nod. "Okay," I say.

Meredith pushes back from the table and lays a hand on her stomach. She's showing.

"What are you reading?" I ask. I turn the page of my paper.

"This," she says. She shows me the cover. It's a book of names. "I'm looking for the baby," she says. "What should we call it?"

"Not sure," I say. I don't look at her. I set down my paper. I get up from the table and head out of the room. She says my name a few times, but doesn't dare come after me. She knows I think the baby's not mine. She's seen the mustaches tagged on the fetuses in her baby books.

Leroy's drunk. He sits in his favorite chair dressed in a blue bath robe. His eyes are red. They glisten. He asks for another bourbon. I take his glass, freshen it, and set it back in his hand. He swirls the glass. The liquor laps against the ice. He looks at the shotgun that leans against the sofa.

"You'd do it if I'd raised you better," he says.

"No," I tell him. "Not true."

Leroy takes a sip of bourbon and exhales slow. I can smell his age. I can taste his drunk.

"You peed yourself at your daddy's funeral."

"I remember," I tell him. I rub my chin and look at the carpet. There's a brown-crumbed stain near my shoe.

"You know how often I pee myself?" he asks.

I shake my head.

"Every day," he says. He throws open his robe. His pale belly hangs over a wrinkled diaper.

"Looky there," I say and smile. "When'd you start wearing those?"

He coughs. "Don't be cute." He sips his bourbon. "I'm a giant infant."

"Seems it," I say, and drag my shoe across the crumbed stain. "Look at this place. Doesn't housekeeping come?"

He grumbles. He stirs. "Used to," he says. "But I learned my lesson." He closes his robe.

"What lesson?"

"They stole from me."

"Oh yeah," I say. "What'd they steal?"

"Not sure."

"Then how do you know?"

"I can't prove it for certain," he says. "I just don't trust em."

There is a bottle of Oxycodone on the table between us. I pick up the bottle and the pills rattle inside. "Mind if I take a few?"

Leroy sips his bourbon. "Nah," he says. "Knock yourself out."

My tie is tight. No one comes in Bistro Twelve where I manage. I walk through the empty dining room dragging my fingers across the white-linen tablecloths making sure the stemware is spotless. It's hard to tell in the soft light. At each table I drop to one knee and bring the glasses up to my face, holding the glass between my eyes and the light. I roll the stem, eyeing the surface, glancing at the front door, making sure no one has entered, throwing looks at the waiters who lean against walls and chat. I find a glass. A smear of auburn lipstick. Unwashed. Jardon.

I take the glass to the kitchen. The waiters spread as I pass. The Mexican cooks are listening to corridos and laughing. I come to the dish station. Jardon has the place spotless. Not a drop of water. Not a bubble of soap. He smiles at me. I hold up the glass. "Missed a spot." Jardon takes the glass from my hand and squints as he rolls the stem between his fingers.

"Sorry," he says.

"Don't let it happen again," I tell him, and I turn to head back to the dining room.

Then I hear it. The glass shattering against the floor. I feel glass bounce off my pants. I turn toward Jardon.

"Oops," he says. His arms crossed. His face grinning.

Meredith takes my feet in her hands. I'm slouched on the sofa listening to the radio. There's a piano. Faintly. I think. The pills are beginning to kick. The music seems wrapped in cloth. My eyes feel lazy. Meredith smiles and works the butt of her hand into the ball of my foot. I smile too. My lips melt toward my ears.

"You saw him today?" she asks.

"I did."

Meredith takes my other foot. She knows the song. She hums as her fingers flitter across my toes.

"Do you think the baby will play music?" she asks.

I pull my feet from her hands. I push out of my slouch.

"Do you play music?" I ask.

She puts her hands in her lap and looks at the floor. She shakes her head.

"Do I?"

Her head shakes.

"Then why would the kid?"

She looks at me. Her eyes throb in their sockets.

"I don't know," she says. "I don't know."

I met the mustached man once. He had pale hands. Meredith dragged me to a coffee shop where he was playing guitar. At the time I didn't know. He sat on a stool in the corner, his guitar pulled high on his lap, his mustache brushing a black microphone when he mouthed his words. His voice was a dull hiss. His music a sleepy bore. But Meredith's face beamed as he strummed his lazy music. She even knew some of the words. I caught her a few times singing along. She introduced us after his set. He watched her as we shook hands. I looked for a clock, but couldn't find one. "My you're lucky," he told me. "My, my," he said and twisted his mustache. He licked his lips and rocked his head. Meredith disappeared the next day.

Leroy's joints are feeble. They jostle as he moves through the lobby. He pitches and grinds while steadying his weight with a shiny black cane. His face is determined. His pace is slow.

"Is the tuxedo necessary?" I ask.

He sets the cane ahead, drags his feet to it then puts his hand to his chest. "Want it right," he says and gasps for air.

It's slow going but we eventually emerge from the lobby and out onto the street. The wind tosses Leroy's tuxedo tails.

"Where we headed?" I ask.

"Round the corner," he says and gasps leaning his head.

We stay close to Leroy's building. The construction continues across the street. Large yellow machines hiss and beep. Men in orange vests and helmets lean against walls.

"What are we doing, Leroy?"

Leroy smiles. He raises the cane above his head.

I look up. Through the sharp sun I see a tethered baby grand piano held by a crane.

"Destiny," Leroy says, and lowers the cane to the pavement.

"Whose?" I ask.

"Mine." Leroy heads toward the taped-off sidewalk below the piano. I follow.

He gets to the waist-level caution tape that runs the construction's perimeter. He contemplates it. He attempts to bend under it, but his body can't manage. He tries to walk through it, but the tape resists. "Hold it up," he says. I hesitate. "Hold it up Goddamn it, it's not a sin."

"What are you doing?"

"Making things easier for the almighty," he says. He clicks his cane against the ground.

"Fine," I say. I grab the tape and pull it over his head. He walks beneath it, turns, holds his palms up to the sky and tilts his face up toward the piano.

I let the tape drop. I walk across the street to a bench. I sit. I watch Leroy's silly pose. I watch the baby grand dangle.

From the distance I cannot hear the argument. One of the construction workers steps to the curb and speaks to Leroy. He crosses under the tape. Leroy hits the man's shin with his cane. The man grabs his leg where the cane hit and calls for another construction worker. The two men take Leroy by his arms and walk him to the street. Leroy raises his cane at the men. Then he turns and walks toward me. He is comically slow. His face is angry.

"What did you think would happen?" I ask when he approaches.

He sits on the bench beside me and gasps, his breaths seem larger than necessary. "Kersplat," he says, and holds his hand to his chest. He takes a clove from his pocket and lights it. We stay on the bench and watch the crane hoist the piano to a floor high above.

I have to fire Jardon. Some of the cooks say he dropped the glass on purpose. There've been a few tables, so he's busy when I approach him. He's standing just outside the kitchen's back door filling a mop bucket with a hose.

"Jardon."

"Yep, sir," he says and releases the hose. It drops into the bucket.

"We need to talk."

Jardon pulls a cigarette from behind his ear, places it between his lips and lights it. "This about the other night?" he asks.

"I suppose," I say.

Jardon blows a cloud of smoke and grabs a blue-headed mop from beside him. He plops the mop head in the bucket, and thrashes the handle so water slushes onto the asphalt.

"How long have I known you, Connor?" he asks.

I touch my head. "Years," I say.

Jardon blows more smoke. He sloshes more water. I can smell the steamy garbage rotting in the dumpster a few yards away. "That's right," Jardon says. "Years." He lets his cigarette fall from his lips into a puddle of water and he tightens the spigot. "I've known you so long that I know your situation."

I look at him cross. "What situation is that?"

"Well," he says. "I know how your dad died, and how you were raised by that Leroy, and how it probably did you harm."

"How you figure?"

"Well," he says, and sloshes water. "I'm gonna tell you something, but you gotta promise not to tell."

I shake my head. "Only thing I need to talk about's the glass."

"Hey," he says. He pulls the hose from the bucket and flings it to the ground. "You promise or not?"

I look down at the wet asphalt. "Sure," I say. "Promise."

"Good deal," he says. "A couple years back I was down in Mexico surfing. I was down there on a bus, cheaper traveling that way, with a girl that I don't want to talk about, because she was bad news with bad skin. But anyhow," he slushes water, "I was down there on that bus with that girl, and there was a wreck, but I don't actually remember how it happened, because they say that it's like that. They say when the pain is that bad you forget, and we got broad sided, I mean slammed into, and I remember a sound like butterflies and a warmth like blood," Jardon lights up another cigarette. "So," he says and exhales. "The warmth and the sound," he flicks ash, "and all of a sudden I'm in a room with a bunch of brown faced nurses staring at my dick. I mean staring. And then a doctor came in with an interpreter, and they told me that I lost part of my dick in the accident." Jardon grabs the mop handle with his thumb and forefinger an inch from its tip. "Like this much," he says. He takes a deep drag off his cigarette and blows smoke.

"Sorry to hear it," I say. "But you can't go breaking glasses."

"Not done," Jardon says, and he clears his throat. "The main thing you have to understand, up to this point," he says and licks his lips, "is that I lost the tip of my dick in a bus accident, and I was hearing butterflies." He sloshes more water. "But the thing is," he says, "is that I wasn't the only one hurt in the accident, and I wasn't hurt the worst. Not by a long shot. The man who slammed into us," Jardon says and wipes his brow. "He died. So the doctor says to me, through an interpreter of course, he says, *Would you be opposed to having a stranger's dick on your dick?*" Jardon takes a drag off his cigarette and stares blankly into the distance.

"You've got part of another man's dick," I say and shake my head.

Jardon puts his hands on his belt buckle. "If you don't believe it I'll show you right here."

"Nah," I say. "I believe you, but. . ."

"Wait," says Jardon. "There's more to the story."

"More?"

"Sure," he says. "I agreed to the operation, but they didn't give me all that many details. All I knew was that I was missing some dick, and there was a man that didn't need any of his dick, and that they were going to give me a smidge of his, seeing as how he took a smidge of mine," Jardon took a fresh cigarette out of his pack and lit it with his half finished cigarette, then dropped the older cigarette on the ground. "So I go under the knife, and when I woke up my dick was wrapped in gauze, and they said not to mess with the bandaging, as it would upset the stitches, and there was a tube running up my dick so I could pee and it not get infected. And then I left the hospital and flew home." Jardon is quiet.

"That's the whole story?"

"No," Jardon says. "I was pausing for dramatic effect. You see," he says. "I don't care that you know I have two bits a dick. What bothers me is what I saw after I healed," Jardon is again quiet. "Well?" he says.

"Well what?"

"You're not curious?"

"No."

"Come on," he says. "Ask."

"Fine," I say. "What did you see after you healed?"

"Something terrible," he says. "About a week after I got home I peeled off the bandage and there it was. A caramel brown dick head and a red spot the size of a dime on it."

"A red spot?"

"Yeah," he says. "A birth mark."

"What?"

"A birth mark," says Jardon and he raises his left shirt sleeve. "Only thing is, I've already got a birth mark." He blows cigarette smoke toward a purple blot on his forearm.

"So," I say.

"So," he says. "I've got two dicks and two birth marks, and it's affected me bad. A man's only supposed to have one of each. Just like you, Connor, and how you been affected, by having the two fathers when that's one too many."

"I guess," I say.

"Nope," says Jardon. "There's no guessing to it. It's the way it is." Jardon throws his cigarette on the ground and mashes it out with his heel. He steers the mop bucket with the mop handle past me and toward the door. "Now if you'll excuse me," he says, "I need to mop up and do some dishes. But you wouldn't know about that," he says. "Being a fancy manager and all."

The door shuts behind him as he works his way into the kitchen.

"I do dishes," I say, but I'm sure he doesn't hear me.

*   *   *

Meredith comes to the doorway of the kitchen as I wash dishes. She leans against the jam.

"Should I leave?" she asks.

I look at her. "Where would you go?"

I put my hand into the soapy water. I move it slowly, because I know there's a knife.

"I don't know," she says.

"Same place you went before?" I ask. I take the knife from the water, and run a sponge along its edge.

She whimpers and lays her hand against her belly. "Fuck you," she says, but it doesn't sound harsh. She turns to leave. I hear her feet drag. I set the knife back in the water. I look at the refrigerator beside me. There is a picture of Meredith's fetus that she got from her doctor. It looks like a glob of static packed tight against a window. There is a date on the picture. I can't quite remember. I take a marker from my pocket and draw a mustache on the static's face.

They call me and I go. It is dusk and the streets are the color of ash. I've had a pill. So what. I'm driving fine. Parking is a dream. Lines like dirty sugar on the black asphalt. The hospital is pale. Everything pale. The lobby, the elevator, the nurse with the clipboard. It smells like reheated food and Clorox. The air is cold and heavy in my throat. I follow him. The man. The Clipboard. His pale shoes against a pale floor making pale noise. In the room machines hiss and chirp. Leroy lies on white sheets. Plastic tubing disappears into veins beneath his translucent skin. Above a fluorescent light dies. Its haunting chemical death rattle makes everything quiver.

"This is him," the man says.

"Really," I say.

The man shifts in his pale shoes.

"Well I'll leave you alone."

He takes a step back and I look at him.

"How long?"

The man looks at his clipboard. "A couple of days," he says.

I nod.

"Anything else?"

I look at Leroy. I look at the man.

"You a nurse?"

"A resident."

The machines are gasping and chirping and the light flickers above.

"How accurate are DNA tests?" I ask.

The man looks at the clipboard. He looks at me.

"You think he might be your father?"

"No," I say. "He's my godfather. My first one anyway."

"First?"

"Sure," I say. "My father gave me him, and he gave me another."

"I see."

"The second one's dead," I say.

I look at Leroy. The man looks at me.

"Pretty accurate," the man says.

"What?"

"The tests are accurate."

I forgot I'd asked. "Thanks."

"No problem," he says. He taps his clipboard and leaves the room.

I walk over to Leroy. The skin of his face sags from his cheeks. The machines hiss and his chest rises. What hair he has is long. I tuck it behind his ears.

Meredith was gone for two weeks. This is what

I think about as I sip Leroy's bourbon. I found her in the stairwell sitting against the wall when she returned. Her arms hung over her bent knees. Her head bowed toward her belly. I kicked her. Not hard. Just enough so she'd stir. Just on her side, so her head snapped back and her long black hair spilled into her mascara-streaked face.

"What?" she asked. She licked the roof of her mouth.

"You alive?"

She blinked her eyes and rubbed her head until she came to focus. She stood with awkward footing and began to cry.

"Where've you been?"

That's what I asked her. She didn't answer. She only shook her head. I climbed the stairs and she followed. I should have shut the door behind me once I entered the apartment, but I didn't. I left it open and she followed me in.

The attendant to Leroy's building let me up without hassle.

"Just getting some personal effects," I said. I'd never said that phrase before. Personal effects.

The attendant nodded and ran his hand down the front of his red jacket. "You have a key?" he asked.

I showed him the key on my key chain. He nodded and twirled a button on his jacket.

Leroy's bourbon heats my breath. I look around the room. There's not much to take. I put his pills in my pocket. I put his whiskey in my jacket. I grab his shotgun and head to the elevator. I blink furiously as the elevator sinks to the lobby.

The attendant calls to me as I walk toward the exit.

"Sir," he says, and looks at my hands. "I can't let you go like that."

"Like what?" I ask.

"You have a gun."

"Personal effects," I say. "Besides, it's not loaded." I flip the lever and the stock breaks. The barrels lower toward the floor and two brass casings are revealed. I smile. "Well, maybe it's a little loaded."

The attendant clears his throat. He shows me his palms. "There's two chambers," he says.

"Yes," I say.

"There's two shells?"

I look at the shotgun. "Yes."

"Sir," he says, "how much more loaded do you think the gun could be?"

I smile. The attendant leans over his desk and takes one of the shells from the gun. He sets it in front of him on the desk then does the same with the next. He reaches beneath him and comes up with a towel. He points to the gun. "Give it here, son," he says.

"I'm sorry?"

"The gun, son," he says. "Pass it here."

I close the barrel and hand him the gun. He lays it on the towel, folds the towel over twice, then passes a roll of tape down the length of the bundle. The tape pops and cracks as it pulls from the roll. He gets to the end of the towel and tears the tape with his teeth. He taps the bundle twice and passes it back over the desk.

"That's better," he says.

I nod. "Agreed," I say.

I take the shells from the desk and put them in my pocket. I smile at the attendant and head into the street.

It's after midnight when I get back to the

hospital. I expect problems, but the resident's behind the desk with a nurse. They're busy whispering and don't notice me pass. I walk to Leroy's room. I pull a chair near him, sit down, and lay the gun at my feet. The machines make their noise. I take a gulp off the bourbon. I put my hand in my pocket. I roll my fingers across the shells.

What would he say if he saw it? Me with the gun. Drunk. Poison from pills making its mellow course through my veins.

"Too late," he'd say. "Too late."

The resident enters the room. He is surprised to see me and his pale shoes squeal against the floor.

"You're not supposed to be here," he says.

"I know," I tell him. I take another hit of bourbon, pick up the gun and stagger toward the exit.

Clean. I feel clean as the car's tires hit the street. My hand against the wheel, the gravity of home urging me on. Slow blues on the radio, streetlight's glow muting the windshield. The world hums like a dying fluorescent. The crackle. That hiss. Like I'm a warm fetus from Meredith's books. Bathed in pink light, veiny eyes covered with flesh, a see-through skull, webbed fingers. I touch my eyes. They are open. I touch the gun in its bundle. Digging at the tape with my fingers, pulling at the towel and loosening the roll. I take the wheel in my left hand. I put my right hand in the pocket with the shells, "Friends," I say to them. I somehow fumble the shells from my pocket to the barrel. I snap the barrel shut. The metallic chant haunts my ears. I want to hear more. I drive south along the bay. It is late, and the road is empty. I lower my window. The blues screams into the road, the cold salty air fills my car. I lay the barrel of the gun across my left arm and force the mouth of the barrel out the window. I place my index finger on the front trigger. The blues thumps through my brain, a piercing guitar wail bends slow notes as I ease the trigger back toward the butt of the gun. Slow as a sunset. Then. Boom.

The car swerves to the right as the gun kicks across my driving arm, and the air fills with the hot smell of gunpowder. I can taste it in the back of my throat. Clean as chalk dust, and I think about the buck shot raining out across the salt water. I pull the gun back into the car. The barrel burns my hand. I roll up the window. I take deep breaths of the gun-shot scented air. I take another pull from the bourbon. The slow poison rolls inside me. I have one shell left.

I park the car outside my apartment complex and drain the bourbon. The light, brittle. The world swings around me. I grapple for the door handle and fall from the car once it's pulled. I land on the cement, the gun lands on me. I use the shotgun like a cane to help myself up. The street is silent. The only noise is my feet against the sidewalk. There is a donut shop a few blocks away. The air is sweet. My stomach turns.

I head into my building. The stairs fight me as I climb them. I stop where I found Meredith when she came back. I pull out my dick and take a piss on the ground. I lean on the gun. My piss is hot-yellow stench.

I enter my apartment with the gun raised and my middle finger against the back trigger. My feet sound like clock ticks hitting the hard wood. I imagine the see-through fetus in Meredith's belly hears me coming. Perhaps he's put his ear against the womb and is twisting his mustache with his fingers.

In the bedroom. Meredith's asleep. Her slow breaths whisper through the dark. Her belly rises and falls beneath the blanket. I place the barrel against her. My finger is against the trigger. I can smell the gunpowder from the empty shell. I wonder what organs the fetus tries to hide behind. He must be frantic, nervously pulling at his mustache and trying to crawl beneath Meredith's spine.

Meredith stirs a bit, but does not wake. She kicks her feet beneath the blanket and her head moves on the pillow. I think it. A murder spills through my mind, but I don't pull the trigger. I stand for a while with the barrel mouthing her belly. Breathing. Thinking. But not squeezing the trigger.

I know in a few moments I'll put the gun in the closet. Then in a few months Meredith will have the kid and I'll raise it. Maybe I'll get lucky. Maybe I'll die and the job will go to someone else. Or maybe I'll live to be as old as Leroy and my body will fail. When that happens I'll hand Meredith's kid the gun. It will still be loaded, but it won't do any good. I won't raise the kid well, and it won't pull the trigger.

Brian Allen Carr was born in Austin, Texas. His short fiction has appeared in *Annalemma*, *Boulevard*, *Fiction International*, *Gigantic*, *Keyhole*, *Texas Review*, and other publications. He lives with his wife and daughter in McAllen, Texas where he works as an English instructor at South Texas College. He serves as assistant editor of *Boulevard* and fiction editor of *Dark Sky Magazine*. He can be found online at www. brianallencarr.com.